CUPCAKES AND MURDER

A TEMPERANCE MATTHEWS COZY MYSTERY

LITTLE BAKERY COZY MYSTERY SERIES
BOOK 2

LUCINDA RACE

MC TWO PRESS

Editor NN Light/ The Author Buddy
Cover design by Jacobs Ink LLC

Manufactured in the United States of America
First Edition March 2026

Print Edition ISBN
E-book ISBN

1

———————

I stacked the last five boxes of cupcakes on the folding table next to the sidewalk—four to a box, each one frosted and ready to taste. Josie ran up and handed me a sign that read, 'FREE! *Thanks for helping on demo day*'.

With a chuckle, I said, "Nice touch. All you needed to add was: new location of Early Rise Two."

With a grin, she whipped out a sign from behind her back. "I'm one step ahead of you, Temperance. It's time people knew what's next for the bakery. Giving out cupcakes is the perfect way to share the news."

"I put a list of ingredients on the box too in case someone has an allergy to any items I used to bake them."

Josie sank down on the wide porch steps of the Victorian home I inherited from my Aunt Penny. She said, "My feet ache and I'm exhausted. Now that everyone's gone we should sit for a few minutes. Oh, and I called in for a pizza and salad delivery."

I glanced at the large roll-off dumpster in my driveway filled with mountains of debris. It was the remnants from the housekeeper's apartment at the back of my home. "This might be a trend with you being one step ahead of me." I waved to Officer Casey Butler as she strode up the walk. We'd become well acquainted last week during the arson investigation when my bakery was reduced to ash and rubble.

"Casey, care for a cupcake?"

She perused the table. "I don't need four decadent little treats."

I waved. "Take a box. They'll keep for a few days. Just store them in the refrigerator in the box."

"In that case, I don't mind if I do." She picked up a box and crossed to where we sat. "How did today go?"

"Better than I ever expected. Russ Patterson enlisted about twenty volunteers, most of whom were subcontractors he uses. Erik Wool, Van Jonas, and Dave Buckle came to provide any first aid that might be needed. And if that wasn't enough, Renee Santorini from Sassy's Slice made party-size subs for everyone at lunch."

Josie said, "Don't forget Belle Green sent over people from the brewery to help out this morning."

"I'm sorry I missed it." Casey sat down on a lower step. "With all that help it must have made short work out of clearing the apartment." Her gaze slid from one side of my yard to the other. "Where's all the stuff?"

Clasping my hands behind my head, I exhaled. "Most of it was gone as fast as it was carried to the curb. What was left, a man named Jonesy stopped by and asked if he could have the rest. He has a third-hand store in Pine Valley, so I told him to have at it."

Casey's brows knitted together. "What's a third-hand store?"

I smiled. "He explained it like this— since the curb scoopers gave stuff a second life after tag sales, anything overlooked was third-hand. It's an interesting take on household goods, don't you think?"

"Sure. At least you don't need to have anyone haul away what was left," she said.

Josie asked, "Casey, do you want to stay for an early dinner? I ordered pizza and salad."

"That sounds great. I'm off duty tonight."

"Ha, from what we've seen in the last week, you're never really off duty."

She grinned. "Sleep is overrated. There was a scuffle today. Josie, did you happen to overhear what set off Franny and Gloria?"

I said, "Well, Gloria grabbed Franny's arm, and Jacob and Chase stepped in to pull them apart. I'm not sure what the argument was about, but the good thing is the four of them left soon after lunch and in different directions."

Casey asked, "I don't think I know them. Are they local?"

Josie replied, "Chase Clark is Franny's brother, and he and Gloria work at Twigs and Petal Garden Center, a landscaping company owned by Kelly Woods. You might have seen the trucks around; the logo is T&P. Franny works at the garden center too. Jacob's a mechanic at Stu's Garage. To get back to the tussle, I'm clueless about the ladies' argument. I've never witnessed Gloria that angry. Typically, she's mild-mannered."

"I hope they work everything out." A couple of kids on bikes zipped down the street, did a U-turn at the end, and slowly crept by, ogling the cupcakes. "Take a box," I called out.

The one boy wearing a baseball cap said, "My mom said I needed to ask permission first."

"You have permission to take a box of cupcakes as long as you like chocolate."

He nodded and looked at his buddy. "Want some?"

The other boy grinned. "Heck yeah. Thanks, Ms. Matthews."

The ball cap boy waved and took the box. "See ya."

"He knew my name; too bad I didn't know his."

Josie said, "That's Kennedy Moore's son, Billy. He's got good manners. The other boy is Jeff Collins."

"Right, Kennedy owns My Closet. I haven't done much shopping since moving to town but she's got nice window displays," I said.

Josie stood. "Temperance, you're exhausted. I'll get plates and silverware and we can sit on the porch for dinner."

I stretched my arms overhead. "No, let's eat on the deck. My little doxie needs to stretch his legs. Hank's been good but he's had a boring day being stuck in my office and I don't want him up all night looking to play. Besides, with just a few boxes of cupcakes left, maybe they'll go more quickly if we aren't hovering."

"I can pick up the pizza," Casey said.

"Delivery tonight. We were too tired." I opened the door and ushered Josie and Casey inside. Taking one last look at the boxes of cupcakes, I smiled. It had been a great day.

A toot of a horn drew my attention to the driveway—a small blue hatchback parked with its engine running. A pizza slice on the roof confirmed dinner had arrived.

"I'll be right in, dinner's here." I jogged down the steps. "Hey, Gordon." It was ironic he was the pizza delivery guy. He was so thin, it looked like he could eat one a day and still look like a reed.

"Hi Temperance," he pushed a button, the hatch on his car opened, and he got out. "I've got your dinner right here."

"Great, we're starving."

He took in the dumpster. "I heard you're going to reopen your bakery. That's a good thing. It's really popular around town."

"We're going to reopen on a smaller scale, and it won't be for a couple of months. We finished the demo today on the apartment at the back of the house. Hence the dumpster."

"My sister Gloria and her friends Franny, Jacob, and Chase

were supposed to help." His gaze slid to the boxes of cupcakes, and he licked his lips. "Are you selling those?"

"Your sister and her friends did a fantastic job, and the cupcakes are free. Would you like a box?"

"Yes, please."

He took a pizza box and a large paper bag out of the back of the car and closed the hatch, following me to the steps. "Order was paid for and tip included too. But I will grab a box as an added bonus,." he grinned.

I took our dinner order. "Help yourself."

"Thanks, and I'm glad to hear you're not letting a little setback derail you."

I smiled. "Never. Have a great night and enjoy the cupcakes."

"We will." He picked up a box and yelled, "Thanks again." He paused before getting in the car. "You know, I could give a box to Henrietta Woods; she can write a piece for the Oak Hollow Gazette just to let folks know you're a phoenix. She's having dinner with friends at Sassy's. I could give her a box if you'd like."

A little publicity wouldn't hurt. "Sure, take all three boxes, and if you see anyone else you want to give one to, go for it."

"Will do." His long strides ate up the lawn as he walked to the card table. He nodded as he picked up the remaining three boxes of cupcakes and beamed. "Yeah. Temperance Matthews, the phoenix. I like it."

"Thanks again, Gordon."

He set the boxes on the passenger seat of the car and backed out of the drive.

"Well, that's the last of them."

Josie held the door for me. "What was that all about?"

I climbed the steps and went to the kitchen. "You'll laugh. Gordon called me a phoenix, and I gave him the last of the cupcakes to pass out. He said Henrietta might do a write-up on the new location. It's a great idea to let people know what's happening with the little bakery."

Casey held Hank on her lap when we entered the kitchen. "Are you laughing after all you've accomplished today? What are you, a superhero?"

I shook my head. "Gordon Nardin delivered our dinner, and he took the last of the cupcakes to pass out to his friends. Before he left, he said I was a phoenix."

With a grin, she put Hank on the floor. "I'll second that. I've never seen anyone take adversity and turn it around so fast. It's great to see the town rally around you."

"It feels good to know I'm an accepted part of the community." I tapped the center of my chest.

Josie took the bag, which contained the salad. "You had doubts?"

"I'm an outsider. Most people in town, you included, are generations deep. My aunt lived here and I was a summer resident. It's not quite the same."

Casey nodded. "I get it. I grew up in the mid-west, but Oak Hollow residents are pretty welcoming. I'm glad I made the move."

I nodded. Before I could speak my stomach growled so loud even Hank looked up, his ears cocked. Laughing, I said, "Let's eat."

Hank barked and ran to the sliding glass door. Bouncing on his front paws, he gave another excited bark. "Someone wants to go outside."

"Is the fence repaired?" Casey asked.

Her mention of the fence caused my heart to flip in my chest, reminding me of the fire that could have taken everything from me, including my sweet pup. "Yesterday, the fence company finished fixing it. It only involved replacing two panels, so they were able to fit me into their schedule. I have to have a fence for Hank since he hates to be on a leash, and he's a dog built around a nose. If someone were grilling hotdogs in Asheville he'd be gone like a flash of lightning."

Josie laughed, "I've seen him in action, and Temperance isn't kidding." She clapped her hands together and slid them in opposite directions. "Greased lightning."

We sat at the round table on the deck, leaving the slider open for Hank. Despite Casey only knowing us for a few days, sitting there it felt like we'd known each other for years.

"Temperance, are you sorry you left the FBI?" Casey sipped her beer.

Mentioning my former job didn't cause a pang of regret. "Not at all. I'm not tooting my own horn but even when you're good at something, if it doesn't make you happy why keep doing it? Working at the FBI, I felt like I had lost a part of my soul, and the only thing that made me happy was baking. I used to call Aunt Penny every Sunday to tell her what I had baked over the weekend. She's the one who urged me to think about making a change. When she passed away, I had just finished a heart-wrenching case, and I couldn't analyze data objectively after that."

"Do you want to talk about the case?"

I heard the empathy-filled words from Casey, and Josie's eyes were soft with unshed tears. I had never shared with anyone what had happened. I wasn't about to tell my friends how I had failed.

I shook my head. "Not now." Squeezing my eyes shut to blink away the tears, I got up. "Hank, come here, little boy."

He was happily digging a crater near my veggie garden. I gave a sharp whistle and he lifted his head, gave me a side eye, and went right back to digging.

Sinking into the chair, I picked up my wine glass. "The hole doesn't matter, he's having fun. I'll fill it in later."

Casey glanced at Josie and shrugged her shoulders.

"Who do you think Gordon is going to give the cupcakes to?"

"He mentioned the editor of the newspaper. I'm hoping Henrietta will give me a write up about the new location and I'm sure he will give some to his friends too. I'm happy they won't go to waste."

"If there were any left, I would have grabbed them to take to the station."

I slapped the table with my hand. "Dang, I should have dropped them at the fire station. That would have been good. Oh, well, tomorrow's another day that I can bake and drop something to them. Maybe I'll make bread too. They could have it with their dinner. Erik mentioned they never turn down food."

"Didn't you lose your sourdough starter?" Josie asked.

"Yes but I'll make a new starter and by the time I'm baking again for sales, it will be strong."

Casey bobbed her head. "Gordon was right, calling you a phoenix. I don't think there is anything you can't overcome."

"Well, the symbolism of rising from the ashes isn't lost on me, but I'd rather have a different metaphor since I've had two fires within two days. But, only good days are ahead of me now." I picked up my slice of pizza and grinned. "I can feel it in my bones."

Josie held up her wine glass. "We should toast to that."

Casey lifted her bottle, and I did the same with my glass. We tapped them together. "Here's to analyzing the taste of my baked goods and not crime scene data."

Josie said, "To your future baking endeavors."

Casey grinned, "And this cop loves all baked goods, not just donuts."

I laughed. "I'll keep that in mind, Officer."

2

———

*M*y cell buzzed. I scooped it from the nightstand and glanced at the time before checking the text message. "It's five o'clock. This better be important." I rolled over and scanned the message before bolting out of bed. I hit the phone icon and waited for Casey to answer.

"Temperance. Sorry to text you so early, but Sergeant Franklin contacted me, and I thought you'd want to know right away."

A lead weight filled my gut. "What's wrong?"

"Franny Clark is dead. She was found with a half-eaten cupcake. The open box next to her was from you."

"And?" There had to be more than a woman dying eating a cupcake.

"The ME thinks she was poisoned by something in the dessert. They are running tests to confirm."

"What?" Hank jerked his head up from the blankets as I yelled. "Unless she was allergic to the ingredients, my cupcakes weren't laced with poison."

"No one is saying you did it. At some point, after leaving your house and Franny eating it, someone must have doctored it. I wanted you to know before it hits the OHG."

"Just great. I'm sure the Oak Hollow Grapevine is awake and spreading the news that now my baked goods kill people." I sank onto the bed and put my head between my knees, taking several slow, deep breaths to push the light-headedness away.

"Temperance, are you all right? Should I come over?"

I put the phone on speaker and set it on the nightstand. "No need. I'm just shocked. Is there anything I can do to help?"

"I need to know who was around when Franny and Gloria argued. We're going to bring Gloria in for questioning, along with Gordon and Jacob. Franny's brother Chase found her, and he's already told the officers everything he knows."

"Chocolate cupcakes and murder. What's next, Brownies and murder?"

She said, "I certainly hope not, but as soon as you can, call Josie and put your heads together. I'll need everything you can share with me to attempt to wrap this case up quickly. I don't want it getting around town about the cupcake connection. You don't need bad press from this."

"I've enjoyed enough inadvertent bad press to last me a lifetime. The fire and death of Marty Thompson put everyone in town on edge, and then Jonah was attacked. It was just too much." But I understood better than the average person that when murder is on the mind of average citizens, it can create an almost unbearable tension. But this time, the bad news was going to be directed toward me, or I should say, my cupcakes.

"I'll call Josie around seven. If you want to stop over, we can mull things over a mug of hot coffee."

"I'm needed at the scene for a while. I'll confirm with Sarge about sharing some information with you since you saw the altercation which could prove valuable."

This was Casey's way of going by the book while picking my brain. I didn't mind, well not really. I left the bureau so I wouldn't have to deal with unfortunate circumstances. This was different, and my gut told me whoever did this wanted to scare Franny for an unknown reason or hated her so much that they felt her life was worth taking. "I'll be home all day so the door's open."

"Thanks, Temperance. I'll see you later."

The line went dead. I sat on the bed as the night sky went through shades of gray until the first rays of the sun brightened my room. Wrapping my quilt around me, I grabbed my cell and lifted Hank to the floor. He stretched his long body before padding down the stairs after me into the kitchen. I opened the slider, and he dashed out to do his morning business. The coffee pot timer had gone off and thankfully the pot was filled with dark, hot brew.

The grandfather clock in the front hall chimed seven times. Josie would be awake by now. Reluctant to call and give her the news, I watched Hank return to his digging spot, trot around the newly formed mound of dirt - courtesy of me - and do a happy little trot to the house. He quickly settled into his bed and tipped his head to the side as if asking me what I was waiting for.

"Stop pushing, little dude. I'm dialing."

"Good morning, Temperance. You're up and at 'em early."

"Hi, Josie." I leaned against the counter. How do you tell your best friend there was another murder in town, and it looked like your cupcake was the weapon?

"What's wrong?"

I coughed. "Casey called earlier. She wanted me to know that she'll stop by in a bit. I thought you should be here."

"Because?"

I couldn't delay the news any longer. "We have to put our heads together and tell her everything we remember about Franny and Gloria's argument, right down to who witnessed it."

"Because?" This time she dragged the word out letter by letter.

"Franny Clark was found by her brother Chase, dead, with one of my cupcakes half eaten next to her. The ME believes it was poisoned."

"What? You've got to be kidding? How could your cupcake have killed her unless she was allergic?"

I couldn't help but have a smile tug at the corners of my lips. That had been my thought. *We're a lot alike.* "My reaction exactly. Nonetheless, we need to try and recall every detail about that argument before Casey gets here."

"Give me fifteen minutes and I'll be right over."

"Coffee's ready; I'll make breakfast."

"I'm bringing my laptop too. Based on last week, I'm sure we'll be digging into some dirt."

Was that a reference to Franny's job with the landscape company, or just about what I used to do—digging up information on people and places and dissecting clues? Did it matter? I was going to suggest she bring it with her anyway.

"Hank, you need to have breakfast, and I need to get dressed, but not in that order." He gave me a sharp bark, and his tail thumped in his blankets. I rushed up the stairs. It was going to be a busy day.

When Josie arrived Hank danced around her feet. She squatted next to him and rubbed his velvety black ears. "How are you this morning, little man?"

His answer was several licks on her hand.

Placing bowls of fruit on the table, I said, "I made muffins to go with the berries and yogurt."

"Great, I'll pour coffee." She gave me a side glance. "How are you feeling about Franny holding a cupcake in her dying hand?"

"That's quite the way to phrase it but I'm of two schools of thought. One, she died eating something delicious."

"Until someone tainted it."

I nodded. "True, and the other side of me is wondering why the heck use my food as the vehicle to kill her?"

"Could someone be out to add a cloud over your bakery?"

I paused, placing the muffins on a plate. "I've already thought of that but to what end? People showing up yesterday to lend a hand so I can rebuild was beyond my wildest dreams."

"It was very generous of people to help." She picked up the mugs and pursed her lips. "The only thing that makes it seem less gruesome is that it was an opportune food item."

A sharp rap on the back door had me call, "Come in."

Casey strode into the kitchen. "Morning, ladies." She ruffled Hank's fur. "Hello there."

"Coffee?" Josie asked.

"Please." Casey pulled out a chair and sat. "It's been a heck of an early morning. Two DBs in a week is a lot."

Josie glanced at me and mouthed, DB?

"Dead bodies."

"Oh." She handed Casey a mug. "Both are connected to Temperance. Is anyone thinking she did this?"

Casey's eyes widened. "Not likely, and if they are I'll set them straight."

"Thanks for the vote of confidence. I thought you were off duty last night. What can you tell us?"

"I was. The chief called me in since I've had more experience in my previous position."

"Before moving to Oak Hollow?" Josie asked.

"That's right. I moved here for a quieter life. But that doesn't seem to be working out in recent days." She sipped her coffee. "Last night, did Gordon take the last three or four boxes of cupcakes from the table?"

"Three, I had five, but those kids on bikes took a box and you had one." I gripped the edge of the counter. "What if whoever monkeyed with the cupcake that Franny ate tampered with the others?"

"Highly unlikely. Outside her place we found an EpiPen on the ground. My guess is someone came over to enjoy a cupcake after Gordon gave them out. They never took a bite and waited until Franny ate hers before leaving."

Josie slumped in a chair. "For her to die."

"Are you sure?" I chewed my bottom lip. "To know that someone could get sick or worse is…"

"Temperance, stop right there. How many people came over yesterday and ate your cupcakes? No one got sick or worse. This is an isolated incident, but it could cast a shadow over your business. We need to strike fast and solve the murder to prove your food had nothing to do with Franny's murder. Or if it did she had an allergy she ignored."

A slow grin filled my face despite the circumstances. "You are asking for our help to solve the case?"

Casey looked directly at me. "This is a one-off situation. You're the only real witnesses I have and you do have an exceptional skill. It'd be a shame to waste it." She steepled her fingertips together.

"Excellent. We figured you'd need our help. Where do we start?" I asked.

Casey toyed with her mug. "Tell me what you know about Franny Clark. Don't start with yesterday."

"I've seen her around town since I opened the bakery. She wasn't a daily regular, but she came in often enough and was always friendly."

"Was she alone?"

"No, she and Gloria were usually together. That's what made yesterday so odd; the argument was borderline vicious."

Casey's brow arched. "Interesting."

Josie said, "The Clarks are locals. Franny and Chase manage Twigs and Petals Landscaping, and they cross paths with Gloria, who works at the garden center."

"And have they worked there a long time?"

"Since high school. If I remember correctly, the three of them started working there during the summers and part-time during school breaks. Franny has a way with plants and flower beds had a way."

Casey leaned forward in her chair. "Take your time, Josie."

She blinked hard and nodded. "Sorry, we were in school together."

"I understand. There's no reason to rush."

Casey was a good cop but also compassionate and she knew how patience would yield the best recollections from a witness, and right now Josie was the witness.

"Were Gloria and Franny friends in high school?"

"Yes. Franny, Gloria, Seth, Chase, and Jacob all hung out together."

"Was Seth here yesterday along with the others?"

Her brow furrowed. "Not during the argument. He was here early, helping with the demo of the apartment. But I'm not sure where he went or what time."

"Did he return?"

"Not that I recall. People left shortly after lunch. With so many folks showing up to help, it didn't take long to get the kitchen and living room walls bare to the studs. Russ Patterson did a great job rounding up volunteers to make the project move right along."

"Did Russ ask Franny to help?"

I said, "He told me he was going to swing by Twigs and Petals and ask for anyone who could to stop by. The owner, Kelly Woods, gave some of the staff time off to help."

"Was that normal for business owners to let their people off to pitch in for a community event like this?"

Josie said, "It is for Kelly. About ten years ago, one of her greenhouses caught fire, and the town came together to help her rebuild. This is her way of paying it forward."

"What happened with that fire?"

Josie's face scrunched up. "I have no idea, but I'm sure there's a record of it at the station."

"I'll check it out."

"Do you think that old case is connected to Franny's death?"

Casey gave me a long look. "Not necessarily. How old would everyone have been at that time?"

"That group is a year younger than me and I'm thirty-five, so they would have still been in college then. Franny went for horticulture, Chase studied arboriculture, and Gloria was a business major."

"Did Jacob go to college?"

Josie's brow quirked. "No, he went to trade school for auto mechanics. Is all this background important?"

"You said they've been friends for years. To understand how they're connected could be important. As we know, murders aren't random and Franny let the killer into her home to share dessert. He or she was known to her."

"And she was comfortable with whoever it was," I added.

Buttering a muffin, Casey looked up. "What did you say Seth did for work and his last name?"

"It's Armstrong, and he's a salesman for a pharmaceutical company. From what I've heard he's doing well financially. He's building a house outside of town."

"Is he in a relationship?"

"He dated Franny for a long time but they broke up a year ago, maybe more now." Josie shrugged her shoulders. "I think they've all dated each other at one time or another."

I asked, "Was there any indication of the motive at the scene? A note, text message on Franny's phone?"

"We're working to unlock her phone so we should have access soon. Chase has a password list for her devices at his place."

"That's helpful." I leaned back in the chair. "If we focus on the argument yesterday, and no one is currently dating anyone?" I glanced at Josie, who nodded. "Then it's not likely a romantic entanglement issue. So, what's the motive?"

Josie said, "What are the typical motives: revenge, money, or jealousy?"

Casey said, "Or financial gain. At this point, we can't rule anything out. We don't have enough information to go on. Let's talk about yesterday. Josie, when the argument arose how many people were around? Was Seth gone at that time?"

"You already asked that but he was. Oh, wait, no." She shook her head. "Kelly Woods stopped by and was talking to Seth. Jacob and Chase were emptying trashcans into the dumpster, and Franny was sweeping the sidewalk when Gloria walked up to her and grabbed her arm, whirling her around. When they came face to face, their looks could have killed."

"Would you say this was a continuation of a fight or something new, like Franny swept dirt on Gloria's shoes and it set off an altercation?"

Josie shook her head, "Oh, it wasn't new. I noticed they weren't their usual chatty selves during the day, but I figured it was because we were all busy getting the job done."

I said, "At this point the evidence indicates that Gloria's the primary suspect."

Casey nodded. "That's where we stand. Without knowing what the argument between Franny and Gloria was about, we can't move forward."

I asked. "When will Gloria be at the station for questioning?"

"Well, that's a minor hiccup. At the moment, no one can locate her."

Josie said, "She likes to fish. Has anyone checked the river?"

"No, but that's a good idea." Casey tapped out a message on her phone and looked up. "Does she have a favorite spot?"

"I'm not sure, but a lot of us used to drop a line down past the big red bridge. There's a path leading to a sandy beach."

"Will you show me?" Casey asked.

Josie glanced at me and I nodded. "I'm coming too." I wasn't about to miss this.

Hank barked. "Little boy, you're staying home to guard the house." He jumped into the middle of his bed and gave me a side-eye look and grumbled.

Casey chuckled. "Someone's not happy he has to stay put."

"You have no idea." I drained my coffee. "Bottom's up, ladies. We're going sleuthing."

3

———

$\mathcal{J}$osie and I drove in her SUV, and Casey was in her truck. This was better optics for her in case anyone was watching us, seen or hidden. Parking in the turnout was easy since we were the only vehicles.

"Ready Josie?"

She turned in the driver seat and scanned the area. "I don't see Gloria's car anywhere. Maybe I was wrong about her coming here. But it's Sunday and the weather is perfect, I just assumed."

"It's an excellent educated guess. We'll take a walk around and see what we might find. If nothing else we'll catch some vitamin D."

With a chuckle, she pushed open her door. "Leave it to you to try and find an upside."

"It's better than the downside." We walked to the top of the path. Casey joined us.

"Josie, have you noticed anything yet?"

"I'm surprised I didn't see Gloria's car. Who knows, maybe she decided to sleep in today, or she could have gone to work."

"I checked with Kelly Woods on the drive over. Gloria had

the weekend off which was why she was able to help at Temperance's place. An officer's been by her house and no one answered the door so the process of elimination puts us here to start the day."

"Josie, is the beachy spot to the right or left at the bottom of the hill?"

"Take a left, it should appear in about a hundred yards. We'll go through a stand of trees, and then it opens up."

Casey said, "Lead the way."

We navigated the steep decline in a single file. There were a few rocks that resembled steps, and I used them to keep my footing. "What's to the right?"

"A small fishing access. We can check there if nothing turns up at RR."

"What's RR? I asked.

"This fishing spot's called Reel Retreat or RR for short. The other spot is the wormhole."

"Because?"

"You can't cast there; you can only drop a line with a worm and hope for the best, which is why most people don't fish there if RR isn't crowded."

Casey lifted her shoulder. "I don't know these things. I've never fished except at the seafood counter at the market."

I laughed. "I'm with you, but the idea of escaping into nature with the sun and sounds of a lazy river while I read a good book is appealing."

We reached the bottom. I glanced right but followed Josie and Casey to the left. No matter what turned up at RR, I was going to the wormhole, if for no other reason than curiosity of what a smaller fishing hole looked like.

Casey and Josie walked side by side. I kept my head down, moving at a slower pace, scanning the scrubby brush lining the path. The sun warmed my shoulders, and grass crunched under my sneakers. Years of training kicked in. At the bureau I had done a bit of fieldwork, not that I told anyone because it was my secret to keep. I quickly discovered it was a career path that wasn't for me long term. I was comfortable with information analysis. Being out here and searching like this tugged at my gut; what if we discovered something awful? That had happened to me twice. I squeezed my eyes shut behind dark glasses and shook my head, forcing the memory into the recesses of my mind.

"Temperance." Casey clasped my arm. "Talk to me."

Josie's head tilted to the side, and Casey's eyes narrowed. "Did you find something?"

"No. Why do you ask?"

"I was talking to you, and you didn't respond."

My heart thumped in my chest. Would she figure out my secret? There was no way she could. That part of my file was buried long ago. "Sorry." I twirled the end of my ponytail around my finger. Casey wouldn't know that was something I did when I got nervous. "I was concentrating, searching for clues. So far, nothing seems out of place along the path."

She slipped her aviator glasses down her nose and stared at me over the rims. "Are you sure there's nothing more going on?"

I forced a smile to my lips. "Yup, other than that, we need to find Gloria. All good here." My voice squeaked as Josie continued to study me. Thankfully, she never said a word. However, I needed to be prepared for questions that might arise later.

"The beach is just on through those trees." Josie jerked her thumb over her shoulder. "Ready?"

"You betcha." I cringed. That didn't sound like me at all, but I couldn't take those two little words back.

Josie waved us forward and once again I brought up the rear. This time I stopped letting my memories take me back to a time I wished I could purge.

Once we were through the few yards of tree growth there was a stretch of sand. It was just as I imagined. The river drifted lazily by, the sandy beach begged for a chair at the water's edge and I could picture myself here with a book.

"This is picture perfect. Josie, why haven't we been down here?"

With a snort, she said, "Hello, you work seven days a week starting before the sun's up."

She had me there. "Maybe before the weather gets cold, we could come down and chill for an afternoon, sans fishing poles, of course."

Josie said, "We can do that." She jogged across the beach. "Casey, look at this."

We ran to join her and on the opposite side from the trees was a small yellow backpack, a pair of sneakers, a headlamp, a fishing pole and a box of what I guessed was worms.

I reached out and before I picked up the backpack, Casey tapped my hand.

She said, "Don't touch it," and withdrew a pair of latex gloves from her back pocket and pulled them on. Unzipping the bag, she peered at the contents and withdrew a wallet.

Josie asked, "Is it Gloria's?"

She nodded. "Yes, but there's no cell phone or car keys." Scanning the area she said, "I'm going to check around. Josie, can you walk into the tree line, calling for her, while I check the river bank?"

I said, "I'll go back to the wormhole and see if there's anything there." I had a niggling sensation in my gut that there was something to find.

"Good. I'm going to call this in and see when reinforcements will arrive. If you see anything suspicious, call me and I'll come. Don't touch anything. I don't want your prints to contaminate evidence."

Josie and I walked back the way we had come as Casey turned to walk away from us along the edge of the river.

"Do you think they'll bring in divers?" Josie asked.

"It's a possibility unless we find something more concrete

like where Gloria is. Would she have taken off and left her stuff behind?"

Josie shook her head. "I wouldn't classify her as careless with her things, and her wallet was in the backpack. No one would just leave that behind."

She pointed to the rise of the hill. "What's the best way to look for clues?"

"In a grid pattern. Start going from right to left, and when you've gotten to the other side of the trees, walk vertically, leaving small spaces between where you've walked. Oh, and keep your head down."

"Have you done this before?"

Swallowing the lump in my throat, I nodded and walked away. It wasn't that I wanted to be evasive but some things were just too much to share with anyone, even Josie.

Memories flooded back. *Despite solid data, FBI efforts to find him were fruitless.* To relieve tension, I shrugged, pulled my shoulder blades together, then lowered my eyes and walked along the path, inspecting each flower, blade of grass, and the stones that littered the narrow trail. Did anything appear to have been disturbed recently?

Knee-high wildflowers swayed in the light breeze. Looking to the river, down the path, and up to the road, three times I called out, "Gloria?"

Rustling leaves was my reply.

I knelt on the ground. A plastic container with holes in the top lay nestled in the tall grass. I opened it and it contained a bit of dirt and wriggling night crawlers. This is a bait box. It was a potential clue but I wondered how long it had been here. What could I use to mark this spot before continuing down the path?

I withdrew my cell and took a picture, then looked around and saw a fist-sized rock and some twigs. I put the rock at the edge of the path and then fashioned the sticks into an X using grass to tie them together. It was a crude way to leave a marker, but it'd have to do for now. Taking another picture of my handiwork, I sent both images to Casey with a text—*On the path to the wormhole.*

Josie texted. *Not finding anything yet. You?*

I tapped out, *I'm not sure. I'll fill you in shortly.*

Head down, I walked forward. The trees hugged the path now, and I anticipated a clearing ahead, just as it had at RR. The canopy provided a respite from the sun's heat. The sound of babbling water reached me.

Sunlight filtered through the trees onto a narrow deserted strip of beach where a thick log rested, appearing to be a spot for fishing. I took several deep breaths as goosebumps raced down my arms. This remote location would be ideal for filming scary scenes in a movie. "Gloria, are you here?"

Twittering birds and a buzzing bee filled the air. I held my breath as my heart thudded and blood rushed in my ears as I walked to the water, praying I wouldn't find Gloria.

My phone pinged with a text. It was from Josie. *On my way to you.*

Should I wait for her before approaching the water? Chiding myself, "No. You can do this," I pressed forward. "Gloria?"

Reeds grew thickly near the small beach. Those areas would need to be investigated. I grabbed a heavy stick. "Gloria, it's Temperance. We're worried about you. Are you here?"

Talking to the air helped center me, and I focused on the search.

I tapped the reeds on the right, flattening them to the ground. But there was nothing to see. I continued walking along them, and with each step, my chest grew lighter. Nothing. "Gloria, if you can hear me, yell."

Once I had checked the small area, I was up the bank, my sneakers sloshing from the cold river water.

At the log, I turned and looked across the slow-moving

current. It was an idyllic place to sit and contemplate life, preferably without the distraction of a fishing pole.

Sunshine sparkled on the surface of the water in front of me. What was underneath the surface? I waded ankle deep in the water and bent over, my fingertips pushing aside a small rock. Breath whooshed from my lungs. This wasn't good.

Josie called, "Temperance, where are you?"

I lifted my hand. "Over here. Call Casey and tell her to get down here fast. I think I found car keys attached to a key ring that has the Twigs and Petal logo."

She raced to the edge of the water. "Gloria's?"

I tipped my head and squinted my eyes from the sun. "Potentially."

"You sound like a cop."

I straightened. "Old habits resurface from time to time."

Josie had her phone to her ear. "Casey, Temperance has found a set of car keys in the water with the garden center's logo. She thinks you should get here fast." With a nod she said, "We won't move," and stashed her cell in her shorts pocket.

I snapped a few pictures of the keys and inspected them for clarity. Satisfied, I tucked my phone away. "What did you find in the trees?"

"Nothing. The police should do their thing. Have you found anything else?"

Nodding, I pointed to the path. "Maybe twenty feet back there was a bait container. I put a decent-sized rock next to it as a marker."

"Huh," Josie jogged down the trail and then came back. "I don't see it."

I looked at the water. "I don't want to get out in case my movements dislodge the keys, so I'll show you after." Passing Josie the stick I had been using to tap down the reeds, I nodded to the side I hadn't searched yet.

"Any chance you can tap down those reeds to see if you find anything else?"

"Sure. Should I move the stick around as if I was looking for a snake?"

My eyes popped. "I hate snakes. Let's hope there aren't any hanging around."

"Are you kidding, with all the noise we've made? They'd have scattered a long time ago."

Shuddering at the idea a snake could slither out of the scrub and into the water, my heart slowed. "Maybe you should wait."

With a laugh, she said, "Don't worry. I've never seen any down here." She eased the reeds from side to side, walking around the back as I had done. "So far, nothing."

"Walk along the edge of the water and look up the embankment."

She gave me a thumbs up. "You know you're good at this kind of stuff. A cool head, logical mind - maybe you should have stayed with your old job."

"I've been happier baking for the last eighteen months than I was for years. This is what I'm meant to do."

Josie's face drained of color.

"What did you find?"

"What was Gloria wearing yesterday at your house?"

Closing my eyes, I attempted to recall the argument between Gloria and Franny. "She was wearing bright pink shorts, a white graphic tank top, and she had a beige sweat-shirt tied around her waist."

"Was there anything on the sweatshirt?"

"The Twigs and Petal logo. Is that what you found?"

She nodded. "And there's blood on it."

"We have keys and a sweatshirt, so where is Gloria?"

Casey walked up. "Sitting on the bank at RR with the worst hangover of her life."

4

Relief washed over me knowing Gloria was alive. "Where did you find her?"

Casey shook her head. "She was passed out downstream . It took a few tries to rouse her, but when she did, she was mighty confused and complaining of the worst headache she's ever had."

"Was she injured?" I asked

She folded her arms over her midsection. "Apparently. What makes you ask?"

Josie pointed to the bushes in front of her. "I think this is the sweatshirt she was wearing yesterday morning, and it has blood on it."

"Casey, any chance you can look here first? My feet are going to be blocks of ice if I stay in this position much longer and I don't want to move and take the chance to dislodge the keys I found."

"Right. Keys." She got close to the water's edge and leaned over. "That's a good catch. I'm not sure I would have seen the key ring; the surface of the river does a good job of obscuring it."

I squinted as I looked at her. "If it hadn't been for the way the sun hit them, I might not have seen them either."

She handed me her cell and flashed me a smirk. "Would you take pictures? Since your feet are already wet, why do I need to wade in?"

I returned a similar facial expression and she chuckled as I said in a sweet voice, "Happy to oblige, Officer."

I took a few pictures and handed her the cell. She handed it to Josie, who was also standing in water in front of the reeds. "Josie, would you mind?"

"No problem." She took more pictures. Casey handed me a plastic bag and a pair of gloves. Josie asked, "Won't the water have washed away any prints?"

I shook my head as I slipped the gloves on. "Not necessarily. In fresh water, fingerprints can survive for several weeks under the right conditions. It's best not to miss the chance."

Casey pointed to me. "What she said," and laughed. "You ladies are making the investigation much easier so far."

"Don't get too comfortable with us helping. Once reinforcements arrive we'll be relegated to the sidelines."

With a snort, Josie said, "Yeah, that's so not happening."

I plucked the keys from the water and slid them into the bag before handing it to Casey as I waded out of the river. "Casey, when I was following the trail to this fishing spot, I saw a bait container. Did you happen to see it?"

She shook her head. "No. What makes you think it was important?"

Looking down the path I said, "I'm not sure, I found it odd."

"We can look when we head back that way."

"Casey, what are we going to do about the sweatshirt?" Josie asked.

"If you can wait there, I'll run up to my car and get a larger evidence bag. I wouldn't want anything to happen to it if we all walk away." She scanned the pictures we had just taken.

Josie winked, "I'll protect the area." She turned to me. "What are you going to do?"

"Casey?"

She looked up from the cell. "Would you mind going to RR and staying with Gloria? She said she'd wait there for me, but she might talk to you if I'm not around."

"I'll see what I can find out." I pointed to the path. "I'll show you that container. I put a decent-sized rock and some twigs near it to mark the spot." I held up my hand. "Before you say anything, it was all I could find."

She shook her hand. "No judgment here. I like how your brain works."

"Josie if you need me, call."

"Take care of Gloria. I'll be fine."

We set off at a quick clip. As I had when I came down the path, I kept my head down and scanned the ground. It never hurt to check things out in both directions. My rock was up ahead. I pointed to it. "There."

Kneeling on the scrubby weeds, I moved them from right to left. I scooted down the path a foot and repeated the motion. "It's not here."

"Are you sure this was the location?" Casey was looking on the other side of the path.

"Positive. Look at the twigs I intertwined next to the rock."

"Someone must have taken it." She placed her hand over her eyes and scanned the area. "I don't see anyone."

I stood. "Maybe someone was fishing, dropped it, and came back when they realized it was missing."

"We didn't see any other cars in the parking area."

"True, but they could have walked downstream to their car."

She frowned. "Then I would have seen them or at least heard them walking through when I was searching the bank."

Out of ideas, I nodded to where Gloria was waiting. "I'll meet you over there."

We split off, Casey climbed the hill and I followed the trail to the sandy beach. *Why would someone double back to get a bait container and make sure they weren't seen? Or could it be a coincidence, and whoever it was didn't know we were around?*

The air was still. I saw Gloria in the distance in a dark green tee shirt, tan and green checked Capri length pants and bare feet. Her knees were pulled to her chest, and she rested her head on them. "Gloria?"

She lifted her head and gave me a weak smile. "Temperance," she grimaced, "what are you doing here?"

When I reached her I sank to the sand, noticing her shirt was ripped. "We came looking for you." Did she know the news about Franny? Should I ask?

"I'm not sure how I got out here."

I tipped my head and asked, "What's the last thing you remember?"

"Franny called and asked me to come over and have a cupcake. Gordon dropped off a box of heavenly bites. I'm sure you heard us arguing at your house yesterday. We needed to clear the air."

"What did you fight about?"

She shook her head. "Nothing important. Friends can get on each other's nerves, but we'll clear it up today."

"So you didn't go over last night?"

She rubbed her temples. "That's just it, after I said I'd stop over my mind's blank. Well, I remember driving, but I don't know."

"You don't remember arriving at Franny's?"

"No. What I'd like to know is how I got here and how I ended up at the edge of the water?"

That was a question I had too, and where was her car? "Is that your fishing equipment?"

With a quick glance over my shoulder, she nodded. "Yes, but why's it here? That gear should be in the trunk of my car."

All the same questions I had. This must be frustrating for her, or could she be lying?

"Where did Casey Butler go?"

"To her car. She had to get something."

"Oh." Putting her hands in the sand, she tried to push herself to a standing position. With a groan, she dropped back to the beach. "That made my head spin."

"Give yourself some time."

I sent a text to Casey asking if she had bottled water in her car and, if so, to bring some to Gloria.

"Temperance."

I looked up. Van Jones was striding in our direction with Dave Buckle behind him. They each carried plastic cases. "Over here, Van." I stood and brushed off my backside.

Gloria sucked in her bottom lip. "Why are they here?"

"Casey called them to check you out since you have a horrible headache and can't remember how you got here. She thinks you may have been here since last night."

"That makes sense since I can't remember anything. Hi Van, hi Dave."

Van said, "I hear you may have spent the night on the bank, and you have a terrible headache."

"I'm dizzy too. I tried to stand and couldn't because it made me very nauseous."

He opened his case and took out a stethoscope. "May I examine you?"

A hint of color flushed her pale cheeks. "Yes."

Well, that was sweet. Dave wrapped a blood pressure cuff around her right arm as Van listened to her heart, flicked the beam of light in her eyes, and asked her to follow his finger without moving her head. He asked, "Do you know how you got here?"

"No. I was driving to Franny's. The next thing I know, Casey's shaking my shoulder, asking me to open my eyes."

"Do you have a history of migraines?"

"No, maybe it's a blood clot."

"Don't jump to conclusions, Gloria. What did you have to eat or drink last night?"

"Can someone call Franny and let her know I'm alright? She must be worried sick since I didn't show up."

Her voice was steady, she didn't blink and she kept her gaze locked on me. I could tell that Gloria didn't realize Franny was dead.

Van said, "Let's focus on you for a moment, would that be okay?"

"I'm sorry. I can't seem to keep my thoughts straight."

"That's all right, now did your head hurt before you left your house?"

She squeezed her eyes tight as if she was trying to clear the cobwebs. "I had some leftover mac and cheese for dinner and I was feeling good, except that Franny and I argued. I hate when that happens."

I asked, "Do you quarrel frequently?"

"Gosh, no. When we do blow up we go our separate ways and then one of us calls the other and we talk, agree to move on, and we're fine again. I can only think of a handful of times in our lives we've been this upset. It never lasts long, only a few hours at most."

Dave asked her to hold out her arms while Van lifted her long hair off her neck. He gave me a nod, and I took a step closer. Her dark locks were matted with blood from a wound at the base of her skull. My eyes widened. That would explain the headache and loss of consciousness. I snapped a couple of pictures and sent them to Casey. I wish she'd get back, but securing the evidence of the sweatshirt was important, and given that there was blood on the collar and shoulder of the garment, it was easy to see where it came from.

"Gloria, do you have any recollection of how you hit your head?"

Her brows knitted together, and she touched the back of her head where Van had lifted her hair. "What the…" Her fingertips had a small smear of blood. "I don't know." Her lower lip trembled and tears filled her eyes. "What happened to me?"

My gut told me this was related to whatever had happened to Franny. Someone hadn't wanted Gloria showing up at her friend's place. But to attack her and dump her at the river was cruel. She could have died.

Casey ran up. "Temperance, I left a couple of officers processing the other spot. Josie's right behind me. What do you know so far?"

Van said, "She was attacked from behind, which could explain her confusion and the headache. I'd say a mild concussion, but we'll know more once the ER doc examines her. For now, we're going to get her ready to transport." He took a bandage and placed it at the base of her skull then wrapped gauze around her head to keep it secured.

Casey dropped to one knee. "Gloria, you must remember something from last night; even the smallest detail could help us determine who hurt you."

"I got off the phone with Franny and told her I'd stop over in about an hour."

"What time was that?"

She narrowed her eyes. "Around seven. Gordon had dropped off cupcakes, and I was going to get some ice cream. I tidied up my place and backed out of the drive."

"Did you see anyone when you got in your car?"

"Not that I recall, it was dusk."

Gloria glanced at Josie, who had joined us. "Would you call Franny and let her know I'm going to the emergency room? I was supposed to be at her house around eight last night. She must be worried. I don't just disappear like a wisp of fog."

Josie looked from me to Casey. "Should we tell her now or wait until after she gets treated for her injury?"

"Casey," Van said, thankfully breaking the rising tension, "could you finish questioning Gloria at the hospital?"

Standing, she nodded. "Yes. We should get the stretcher down here."

I asked, "How will you transport her up the incline?"

Dave said, "We'll secure her to a backboard and as soon as we get a few more officers here, we'll carry her up." He set off at a fast pace up the hill, which I assumed indicated he was getting the backboard.

"Can we help?" Josie asked.

Casey said, "I'll get the guys."

Josie and I sat on either side of Gloria. She looked me square in the eye and asked, "How do you think I ended up here?"

"I'm not comfortable giving you a scenario that you might confuse with facts."

"So, you have an idea?"

"A working theory." I clasped my hands together and watched the water drift lazily by.

"It's not good, is it?"

I shook my head. "Probably not. Most people don't get thunked on the head and left beside a river."

She placed her cold hands on mine. "There's a bright side, whoever it was didn't toss me in the water. I could have drowned. And who knows, maybe I'll remember something."

That was the double-edged sword. If she remembered and it was connected to Franny's murder, Gloria could be in danger. A shiver raced down my spine. This was too much like Jonah having memory issues just a few days ago. The three of us sat quietly as Van packed up the medical equipment.

Casey and two police officers joined us. Dave returned with Erik Wool and another fireman. Josie and I wouldn't need to lend additional muscle to get Gloria up the embankment and into the ambulance.

She looked at the group gathered around us. "Will someone get my car back to my place?"

Clearing her throat, Casey said, "Your car's not here or at your house."

"Maybe it's at Franny's?"

I heard the hopeful tenor of her voice. Casey and I exchanged an inquisitive glance.

Gloria wrapped her arms around her knees. "I saw that, what's going on? I'm not going anywhere until you start talking. I've asked a few times for someone to call Franny, but you think I didn't notice that you never answered me and the worried glances you exchanged? Will you please call Franny?" She turned to Josie. "Please. You know she's a worrywart."

Josie rubbed the back of her neck. "Casey?"

"Gloria, I'm sorry to tell you. Franny was discovered very early this morning by Chase. She died at some point during the night. We believe she was murdered."

Her eyes widened. "Temperance, that's not possible."

5

———————

$\mathcal{W}$hy she looked at me was surprising. I wasn't a police officer, even if she knew about my former life; that was the past. I was reopening my bakery. Coming to the river today was a favor to Casey.

"Gloria, Casey and the other police officers will find out what happened to Franny and to you."

"But Temperance, everyone in town knows you were instrumental in figuring out what happened to your bakery. Even before you were forced into the woods," she shuddered, "you worked for the FBI."

"That's the past." I glanced at Casey. "Please reassure Gloria that you'll take care of everything?"

With a curt nod, Casey said, "I promise we will get to the bottom of this situation and justice will be served."

"And you won't stop?" Her voice quivered.

Placing a comforting hand on Gloria's shoulder, she said, "Never."

Van crouched next to her. "We need to get you out of here. Are you ready?"

She nodded and placed her hand in the sand to push herself up.

"Gloria, we're going to lift you onto the board. You won't need to do a thing. Once you're lying flat, we'll strap you securely to it and you'll be in the ambulance in no time at all."

"If you hold my arm, I'm sure I can walk."

Van said, "No, it's safer this way. I wouldn't want to take the chance of you losing your balance and falling."

There was a firmness to his voice that seemed to comfort her.

"All right. What do you need me to do?"

He nodded to Dave as he placed the board next to Gloria. "He'll get your feet, and I'll support your shoulders and head. We'll ease you over the sand onto the board. If you get dizzy, give it a moment before you lay down. Then we'll put the straps on and get you on your way."

Her voice was soft. "I'm ready."

On the count of three Van and Dave placed Gloria on the board and secured her. Erik and the other officers and fireman stepped in, each taking a handle. Walking in sync they crossed the trail and scaled the steep incline. Casey followed them up the hill. Josie and I remained at the base watching until they were out of view.

She turned to me. "Should we poke around a bit before we head home?"

I frowned. "Yes, let's walk the shoreline in the direction that Casey discovered Gloria."

Falling into step, we walked with our heads down. I wasn't sure we'd find anything but it didn't hurt to be vigilant. Crossing the beach, we walked downstream. The current of the river increased as the width narrowed.

"Do you think whoever attacked Gloria was hoping the current would take her downriver? There are some waterfalls up ahead, maybe less than a quarter of a mile."

I tipped my head and looked upstream. "Casey didn't mention finding her in the water, just at the edge. But it's possible she might have pulled herself out. It could have been cold enough to rouse her." I stuck my hand under the surface. The flow was stronger here. "If someone hoped for her to get washed downstream and drown, that's attempted murder. The head wound could have been attributed to her hitting the rocks."

"Why was she attacked at all? Don't you agree it must relate to Franny's death?"

"I'm sure it is. Two friends are getting together for dessert after an argument that several people witnessed. One ends up here and could have died; the other is dead. We need to reconstruct the argument from yesterday and remember who was still at my house. We might have overlooked someone. That's a critical clue."

"Too bad you don't have security footage like when the bakery burned."

I nodded. "I turned the cameras off so they wouldn't ping all day with everyone moving around and I didn't turn them back on until after dinner last night."

"That's unfortunate."

We walked a few more steps to where the scrubby grass was matted to the ground. "This must be where Casey found Gloria." I took several pictures of the spot and the surroundings.

"It's close to the water. Were her clothes or shoes wet?"

"She was barefoot and her clothes appeared to be dry. I wouldn't necessarily expect them to be wet if she was dumped here around eight, which is a rough estimate on my part, since she said she was supposed to be at Franny's by then. The shock of the water might have been right after."

"Right, saving herself from drowning." She shuddered. "It's so hard to think about."

"Then don't. At this time we don't know what someone's intention was. They could have put her here to keep her out of the way and without a car she might not be able to walk home in the dark, especially with a head injury."

"I'm going with your theory. It wasn't meant to be murder."

I squeezed her hand. "Learning about one for today is more than enough. Gloria evaded the question about the argument. Why do you suppose that is?"

"Well, she didn't know Franny was dead yet, maybe now that she does, she'll share the details with Casey."

"Temperance!" Casey jogged toward us. "Anything new?"

"No. Is it okay if we go back to the worm hole? I want to take one final look since I spent most of the time in the water."

"Sure, I'll go with you."

Josie asked, "Did Gloria say anything about Franny?"

"No. Between her head injury and the shock, she was staring at nothing when they loaded her into the ambulance. I'll need to get to the hospital in a bit, but there's no rush since the docs need to check her over. I'm sure they'll scan her head to make sure there's no swelling on the brain. That gash looked deep."

"Has there been a report yet on her car?"

"Not yet. I put out an APB since I'm guessing she was attacked after she got in the car. Then the attacker drove her vehicle away and dumped it."

"Before going to Franny's," I concluded.

She gave me a sharp look. "You agree the incidents are linked."

I nodded. "I'd be shocked if they aren't."

"Me too."

Josie said, "I agree as well, but what the heck? This means once again someone we know is a horrible person."

I said, "Good people can make very bad decisions. Don't start looking at our friends and neighbors as if everyone is a bad seed."

A mask slid over her face, and I knew by the way her eyes

rounded and filled with tears she wanted to cry. "Josie, Casey will arrest the guilty person."

She nodded. "I know it's just…"

I hugged her. "I get it. We can help the police by doing what we can, keep a sharp eye, talk about clues and pass information to Casey."

"Then let's do this."

I grinned at the determined set of her jaw. "Casey, you heard the lady. Wormhole time, and then by any chance can we go to Franny's house?"

"I knew you'd want to swing by the scene, and I've cleared it with the sarge. He wanted me to pass along and that he'd welcome your input."

"That's good to hear. Most times amateur sleuths aren't welcome at crime scenes."

Josie snorted. "Whoever said you were an amateur?"

Casey laughed. "Good one, Josie." They slapped each other high five.

AFTER WE SEARCHED the area where we discovered the keys and the sweatshirt, Josie and I followed Casey to Franny's house. It was a small cottage on the outskirts of town, closer to Twigs and Petals garden center.

"I've been wondering about the sweatshirt. Why get rid of it upstream? Why not leave it on Gloria? It would have helped her stay warm overnight."

Josie glanced at me as her hands tightened on the steering wheel. "I hadn't thought of that.

How do you think Franny died?"

"Casey mentioned an E-pen found outside the house. She must have ingested something she was allergic to, injected herself and went back inside for the medicine to work."

"Then she died from anaphylactic shock?"

"Hypothesis only at this point. Did you know if she had health problems or an allergy?"

"No. We weren't super close, so she could have developed an allergy recently and I wouldn't have known. Gloria would."

Josie pulled up alongside the lawn. Police cruisers were parked in the driveway. Casey parked behind one. When I got out I stood next to the car looking up and down the street, noticing the stubby shrubs in front of Franny's home, the broken light fixture at the front door. The screen was shut but the interior door stood open.

Josie came around the front of the SUV. "What is it?"

"The house is neat and tidy, so why would she have left a broken light at her front door?"

"She wouldn't, she was fastidious about her house. When she had a housewarming party after she bought it, everything was perfect inside and out."

"Come on, Casey's waiting for us near the garage."

As we crossed the grass, I noticed several people were huddled together at a neighbor's house across the street. "Do you know who they are?"

Josie glanced behind us. "Jacob Heffin's mom, Babette, and his grandma, Hattie. Also, I think it's Taylor White from the laundromat. But she doesn't live in this neighborhood. Don't look now, but they're pointing at you."

"Oh I'm sure word got out that Franny had a cupcake in her hand and now they're all thinking I caused her death." When Josie didn't correct me, I knew I was right. How was I going to get people to buy my baked goods if they all thought I was the harbinger of death?

"Don't worry about them. I never saw Jacob's mom or grandma in the bakery."

"Thanks." Near the front step was a solitary yellow cone. Then another under the light fixture. The investigative officers must realize that it was probably the result of the attacker's actions either before they entered or when they left.

Sergeant Franklin came from the side of the garage. "Temperance, thank you for coming by." He held up his hand before I could remind him I was retired. At least that's how I wanted to think about leaving the bureau, and not that I was a quitter.

"It's good to have an extra set of eyes," he smiled at Josie, "Or two."

"Can you share any details with us? I know most of what you have is confidential."

His brows knitted together. "Casey mentioned you know about the medication dispenser we found," as he gestured to the one small cone. "We won't know until the autopsy is complete the exact cause but a healthy young woman doesn't just drop dead while enjoying a cupcake. Especially not one of yours, Temperance."

"Thanks for the vote of confidence." I bobbed my head toward the group closely watching our every move. "I get the feeling they wouldn't agree with you."

"Never mind those busybodies. They need to have something to talk about during the excitement. Now when we arrived on the scene, Chase was inside the house performing CPR on his sister."

"Was there any chance it would have worked?"

"Based on the ME's initial exam, he thought she died somewhere between nine pm and midnight."

"What time did Chase arrive?"

"He said six-thirty. They planned to go for a run this morning at six and when Franny didn't show up at his place and didn't answer, he grew concerned and came over. That's when he saw the front door was open. He entered and discovered her sprawled across the sofa."

"Has she been removed?"

He dropped his chin. "Yes. Everything else is the same. Do

you want to look around?"

"Please."

"Do you mind putting booties over your shoes and slipping gloves on? I don't want to take the chance of cross contamination."

"Not a problem."

Josie said, "Is it okay if I come too?"

"Of course, as long as you don't mind the stipulations?"

"I'm good."

Casey held out shoe coverings and gloves to us. "Put these on at the door, and we'll go in through the garage entrance."

We donned the booties and I held the gloves in my hands.

She said, "I'm not going to give you any details, but feel free to have a running commentary while we're inside. Even the smallest thought could be important."

Josie said, "I've been here a few times so I might be able to tell you if something is out of place or amiss."

"Exactly the type of details I'm interested in."

I said, "I've never been here so you'll have opposite ends of the spectrum."

"Josie, would you know if Franny had any health concerns or allergies?"

"Not that I'm aware of. As I told Temperance, we were friendly but not close. Not since school, anyway. You know how it goes. We all took different paths. I attended art school, and she studied horticulture. I couldn't even tell you where she went. We lost touch for about five years. But ask Gloria or Chase. They would know."

"That's good information, thanks." Casey pushed open the breezeway door. To the right was the garage and the left was the kitchen.

"Kitchen first?"

I nodded and pulled the gloves on, as did Josie. We didn't want to accidently touch a surface and leave our prints.

Inside on the counter was a set of car keys, a brown

leather wristlet, and a folded light green sweatshirt with the Twigs & Petals logo. "Are these Franny's?"

"Yes," Casey said.

Plates and wine glasses were in the dish drainer and the coffee pot was full. It must be on a timer. The white cardboard box sat on the counter, containing one cupcake. I glanced around. "Is it okay if I go to the living room?"

"Sure."

I stood in the archway. On a small round table, next to an armchair, was a plate and a cupcake liner, with a few crumbs and an empty mug. Beside where Franny's body was discovered was an identical plate and a half-eaten cake.

"So if Gloria hadn't arrived, who ate the other two cupcakes and where's the other liner?" I turned in a circle. Nothing was out of place.

Josie called to me from the breezeway. "Temperance, you need to see this."

Driven by the urgency in her voice, I strode through the kitchen into the entryway. The garage door was open. Inside were two vehicles. One was a small SUV that had the T & P logo closest to the door, and the other was a dark maroon Subaru hatchback. I pushed the garage door button to open it and walked around the back of the car, studying the cement. Tiny drops of congealed blood were near the car door, but I couldn't tell if they were leading to or from the car.

"Who does this car belong to?"

6

C asey said, "We believe Franny had a work vehicle and a personal car."

"Did anyone check the registration?"

Josie stuck her hands in her pockets. "Well, she didn't own a Subaru. The other car is Gloria's." Shaking her head, she asked, "Why didn't someone run the plates?"

It was a fair question, and one Casey didn't take kindly to by the scowl on her face.

"The first concern was for Franny's status and getting a statement from Chase. I know it feels like we've been at this for hours but the events of the morning have moved very quickly. Chase arrived at six-thirty. He called 9-1-1 fifteen minutes later. I was called at seven and then contacted Temperance; since then, we've been working on two cases. It's not like we deliberately overlooked critical information."

"Casey, I'm sorry. I didn't mean anything by what I said; this is just distressing."

The driver's window was down. Blood was on the headrest. "Casey, the attack happened when she was in the car. Look, there's blood on the headrest."

She came over and pulled open the back door behind the

driver's side. Using her flashlight she scoured the interior. "That is a lot of blood. I don't see a weapon."

"Since Gloria's keys were in the river along with her sweatshirt, I'm guessing the weapon is long gone and the sweatshirt was used to keep blood off whatever vehicle was used to transport her to the river since she couldn't be found here."

Casey mused. "They probably meant for the sweatshirt and keys to be taken by the current." She stepped out the door. "Sarge, has anyone looked over these cars?"

"Not yet. Why?" He walked over.

"Josie has identified the Subaru as Gloria's and Temperance found blood. We can assume Gloria was attacked here."

He gave me a hard look. "Don't think we're incompetent. In addition to this crime scene, we had Gloria's issue, and someone broke into Twigs & Petals too. The department is stretched thin this morning."

That was a twist I wasn't expecting. "The garden center? Was anything taken?"

"Kelly Woods is talking with a couple of officers at the landscape office. She's closed for the day until we can get more cops over there to survey that scene. To be honest, I was more worried about vandalism."

"So she's found nothing so far?"

"Correct." He waved to an officer striding up the sidewalk. The approaching officer had been at the river. "Benson, check out the Subaru. It's Gloria Nardin's."

He gave me and Josie a nod. "Sure thing, Sarge."

Casey said, "I'm going to call Ms. Woods to ask why Franny would be driving a company vehicle."

I looked between the sarge and Casey. "Is it okay if I go back inside and look around a bit more?"

Sergeant Franklin nodded. "If you see anything suspicious, let me or one of the other officers know."

Josie and I entered the kitchen and once again scanned the

space. *Buzz. Buzz.* There was a bee bumping into the kitchen window.

"Josie open the door, I'm going to see if I can show this guy outside." I picked up a small notepad from the counter and waited until the back door was propped open.

"Be careful," Josie said.

"Don't worry, he'll be buzzing around the flower gardens in no time at all." My first attempt to get him flying out the door proved unsuccessful. All I got was an angry buzzing sound for my effort. It was now bumping into a cabinet door. "Keep an eye on the bee. I'll open the window and screen."

"Just squash it."

I smirked. "I won't be responsible for the dwindling bee population. Besides, it won't sting me unless I swat or step on it."

She stood away from the open door. "Ugh, I've always been afraid of those little buggers."

Once the bee cooperated and flew out the window, I pulled the screen down, locked the sash, and Josie closed the door. Diversion over, I was ready to take one more look before we went back to my place.

I set the pad on the counter and a slip of paper dropped on the floor. I picked it up and read it. "Call doc about more EpiPens." I looked up. "She must have a severe allergy to need more EpiPens." I set it on the counter to pass it along to the officers for follow-up. Once they determined what her allergy was, I could compare it to the list of ingredients I had used in the cupcakes. My gut sloshed like a washing machine as my mouth went dry. I must inadvertently be responsible for Franny's death.

Josie said, "Stop. I know what you're thinking. I saw the ingredients listed on the boxes. If Franny was allergic to something you used in baking, it was her responsibility not to eat them."

The logical part of my brain agreed, but my heart ached. "I know, but it doesn't make this any easier."

I walked through the rest of the home. Josie had been correct. Franny was fastidious about keeping things tidy. When I entered the bathroom, I noticed the medicine cabinet door ajar and the drawer on the vanity was shut all the way. "Casey?" I snapped a few pictures on my cell phone.

Who had been searching and for what?

She came around the corner. "Did you find something?"

I pointed to the door and the drawer. "I haven't opened them, but I thought you might want to take a couple of pictures, and then we can look inside. The rest of the house is tidy, so it doesn't jibe with the rest of the place. I wonder if the killer was looking for something specific."

"I appreciate you waiting." She took several pictures and glanced at my hands.

Holding them up I said, "Gloves are still in place."

She smiled. "Making sure we're compliant with procedure." The drawer was first. Bottles of nail polish, dental floss, and makeup brushes were lined up in an organized fashion. Next, we looked in the cabinet. Toothpaste, a couple of bottles of over-the-counter pain relievers, bandages, and a tube of mascara filled the shelves. The bottom shelf was empty, but where were the former contents?

I snapped a couple more pictures, and Casey did the same.

Josie stood in the doorway. "The bedroom is tidy, not so much as a speck of dust on any surface. I wish I had Franny's devotion to cleanliness." Her face drained of color. "That was in poor taste."

I wanted to wrap Josie in a hug. Maybe I shouldn't have brought her to the murder scene, but she had a keen eye and had been useful last week when I was following clues about my fire. "I'll bet Franny would be pleased to know that someone appreciated her efforts with her home."

"I hope so. It's no disrespect on my part."

"Ladies, if there's nothing left for you to look at, I'm going to hang around. I'll stop by when I have a bit more information that I can share but it won't be until later. Next I'm headed to the hospital to check on Gloria."

"Sounds good."

Josie said, "Tell her if she needs anything to call." She pointed to the front door. "I'll meet you outside."

After Josie walked away, I asked, "Are they rushing the autopsy report to see what caused Franny's death?"

"They are, and I've reached out to her primary care doctor to see what the EpiPen was prescribed for which may help us determine the cause of death even before we get the report back. He hasn't returned our calls yet but it's just a matter of time."

"Good. You know where I'm headed."

Casey asked, "What are you going to research?"

I quirked a brow. "What makes you think I'm opening a laptop?"

She shrugged. "It's how your brain works."

"True, but when Josie and I get back to my place, we're going to reconstruct the argument, see if we can remember who was where. My gut is telling me that the confrontation was the catalyst for the murder and attack on Gloria."

"There's no evidence to suggest Gloria was here other than her car and the blood trail."

I pursed my lips. "She wasn't the person who sat in the armchair." It wasn't a question but more of an observation.

"She was hit on the back of the head while in her car. The blood spots were only near the car door; it wasn't like there was a trail from the kitchen door to it."

"Gloria wasn't running from the house to her car in an attempt to flee. She had to have been in the car when she was struck." I hurried through the house back to the garage. Officer Benson was taking photos of the scene.

"Officer, did you find any bloody fingerprints inside the car, specifically on the driver's door handle?"

He glanced at Casey, who nodded. "Sarge wants Temperance included in this case. Former FBI."

His eyebrows flashed up and held as he focused on me. "The only blood found was on the headrest and behind the driver's seat. There's nothing on the door or dash."

That matched with my working theory. She didn't get out of the car on her own steam.

"There are a couple of bloody rags under the car. It looks like someone tried to clean up."

I crouched down. "I don't see any smears near the drops of blood."

Benson pointed to a smear that was just visible under the car. If I hadn't been looking where he pointed, I would have overlooked it. "It's easy to miss it. I discovered it when I sprayed Luminal."

"Any theories for what happened here?" Casey asked.

"Someone could have gotten into her car before she arrived here. She might have stopped for gas or at the convenience store and that's when they got in. But why was she attacked? To prevent her from going into the house would be my guess."

I snapped my fingers. "Gloria said she was going to pick up ice cream on her way over. Did you find an ice cream container?"

"There was a cooler bag on the passenger seat and a pint of melted rocky road ice cream was inside."

"Was there anything else in the vehicle?"

He shook his head. "That's it."

I looked at Casey. "If Benson is correct and someone got into her car at the store, were they a part of the events and was this planned? Could Franny have already been dead or dying when the attacker intercepted Gloria?"

My head spun with so many questions that were all part

of a very confusing web of data. At this point nothing was clear in my head. I needed to create a list of the timelines as they might have happened, starting with the fight between the ladies at my place and moving it forward to when Franny died and Gloria was attacked. One thing I was sure about was that Gloria hadn't clonked herself in the head, left her car in this garage, and walked to the fishing spot to collapse on the bank—two different but connected crimes.

"We don't have a motive," Casey said. "These are two local women who work in the landscaping and plant world. You don't make enemies because of shrubs and grass seed."

I gave her a stern look. "You never know what is going to trip someone up and have them go down a dark path."

"True but this is Oak Hollow, a sweet small town where people actually like each other."

"Casey, I know that's why you moved here, to get away from senseless crimes. But we both know under every shiny surface can hide more sinister actions."

What I wasn't about to say was that it was one of the main reasons I chose to relocate here other than the fact that I had inherited Aunt Penny's house and it was time to leave my day job. Dissecting clues for horrendous crimes had almost damaged my soul beyond repair.

Her cell rang and she answered it. "Officer Butler." She nodded. "Okay, I'll be there in fifteen. Thank you." She said, "Gloria's been discharged from the hospital. Apparently, she called Chase and he's going to stay with her for a day or so just to make sure she's okay."

"That's nice of him. I didn't realize they were close."

"It's his sister's best friend. I'm going straight to her place to question her again. I hope she remembers something that can help us."

"Are you going to tell her you found her car?"

She exhaled. "I'm not sure what I'm going to say. Is she deliberately repressing what happened last night, or are her injuries causing the memory loss? Either way, it will be tricky."

"Is it possible Chase noticed her vehicle in the garage?"

"Another good question. I'm going to check in with Sarge before I take off. I want to be there when they arrive. With some luck, I can look around her place while I'm there."

"Do you want company?"

She shook her head. "Not this time. What I need is to understand that argument and who was around. If you and Josie can reconstruct the event and pinpoint the players, that would go a long way in solving this puzzle."

"Okay. You can count on us." I exited the garage and looked at the ladies still standing across the street. Making a split decision, I detoured in their direction.

Taylor whispered something behind her hand, and Babette nodded. Hattie stepped forward.

"Can I help you, Temperance?"

"As a matter of fact you can. I was hoping you might have seen some cars coming or going last night at Franny's place."

Hatti said, "Sergeant Franklin already asked us. If you want to know, maybe you should conversate with him."

"You might have told him something, but what I'd like to know is what you didn't tell him."

They looked between each other and Hattie said, "Just that we think Franny had a new boyfriend but was keeping him a secret, or she had more than one visitor last night."

7

———

After Hattie dropped her little bombshell about Franny's new boyfriend and that she had company, they didn't have anything else to share. That was after they reassured me they didn't think my cupcakes had killed Franny. As far as they knew she didn't have food allergies. They had each enjoyed a little cake at my place the day before when they stopped to peruse the curb items.

"Temperance," Babette said, "Don't worry about the Early Rise part two. No one will ever believe you had anything to do with this unfortunate incident."

I wanted to ask why she thought this was just an unfortunate incident, but everyone deals with tragedy in their own way. Maybe Babette's was to downplay events. I let it go.

"If you think of anything that the police should know, tell them right away. For the town's sake, we need to get the guilty person or persons behind bars."

Taylor's mouth went slack. "Do they think there's more than one person involved?"

That got her attention. I held back the satisfaction I felt. "We just don't know. Anything is possible. Take care, ladies."

I could feel the weight of their stares as I strode across the road to Josie's SUV. I gave her a wink. "Let's go."

She got in and glanced my way before pulling away from the curb. "Did you learn something?"

"I did. Franny had a boyfriend."

"Really, I haven't seen her with anyone since she broke up with Seth Armstrong. They dated for a long time, but it's been over for months."

"Hattie didn't want to mention who it was but I'm sure she knows exactly who it is. Why do you think she wouldn't say?"

"Good question. It might be that she thinks the person doesn't have anything to do with Franny's death and doesn't want to point a finger at him."

"Franny was comfortable enough to let this person into her home." I watched out the window as we drove through town and turned down Spruce Street. My large Victorian was at the end across from Green Stride Wood, a nature preserve. A work truck with the RP logo was parked in front.

"Russ is here." Josie turned into the drive and parked.

I got out and my friendly contractor, with molten milk chocolate eyes, came from behind the garage.

"Hi Temperance. I hope you don't mind me stopping by. I tried to call but you didn't answer. I wanted to measure for a couple of damaged trim boards that you need to replace from the fire."

"Not a problem. I just need trim boards?"

He nodded. "Yeah, the clapboards are fine but the trim was singed a bit and rather than patching, which could lead to rot down the road, it's best to start with good boards."

"Do you want to come in for coffee?"

He smiled at Josie. "If you ladies are busy, I can take a rain check."

She smiled. "Come on in. We've had a busy morning and could use the break."

I was hoping to question him about yesterday. Maybe he noticed something amiss between Gloria and Franny. The best way to find out was over coffee and a muffin.

"Great. Let me put my tape measure back in the truck and I'll be right in." He jogged down the driveway.

Josie watched me watch him. "He's handsome."

I felt heat flush my cheeks. "That's not why I asked him to stay. He might have noticed something yesterday."

She smirked. "If you say so."

At a loss for words, I hurried up the back steps and inside. Getting the coffee ready, it felt like we had left this kitchen a week ago with all that had happened. Josie set the cream, sugar and mugs on the table. Russ tapped on the door before entering, his smile wide and a twinkle in his eye. He held out a bakery box and flipped back the top.

"I hope it's okay. I stopped at the donut shop and picked up some goodies."

My mouth watered when I saw Boston cream, powdered jelly, maple frosted, and apple fritters. "You went to Asheville for donuts?"

"It was no big deal. I had time."

I took the box and gestured to the kitchen chairs. "The coffee will be ready soon."

"So where were you ladies off to bright and early this morning?" He looked from me to Josie and back. "Did I say something wrong? Temperance, that line between your eyes appeared, and you looked at Josie with your head tipped, as if asking her a question."

"I'm surprised you would know our facial expressions."

Josie snorted but coughed to cover it up.

I scowled at her as Russ rubbed his hand over his face. His cheeks flushed deep pink. It was sweet that he blushed, and maybe there was some truth to what Josie had said.

"Well, we've been friends for a while now and I've noticed a few expressions, that's all."

We needed to get off this topic. As he shifted in his seat, I finger-combed my hair and adjusted the neckline on my T-shirt.

"I know this will have hit the town grapevine but what we talk about here, can you keep it confidential?"

His eyes widened. "Of course. I won't say a word."

"Franny Clark was found by her brother, Chase, earlier this morning. She was dead."

Slack jawed, he said, "What? That's awful. I had no idea she was sick."

I averted my eyes. Took a deep breath and said, "She wasn't. It was murder."

He went utterly still. "Franny. Dead. Murder."

"There's more."

Josie nodded. "We're hoping you might be able to help us with something that happened yesterday."

She was right. I said, "Gloria Nardin was initially a person of interest since she and Franny had an argument late morning out in front of the house. When the officers went to question her, she wasn't home. Josie suggested she had gotten up early to go fishing since everyone knows it's her favorite hobby."

"You went to RR?"

"You know the nickname?"

He grinned. "Of course, and the wormhole, too."

"Yessss." I drawled out the s just for a bit of levity since what I was going to say next was anything but. "We discovered Gloria at the edge of the water downstream from the beach. She had a head wound on the back of her head and was unconscious. Currently, she's in the emergency room, but she'll go home today. Chase is going to stay with her." I omitted talking about the keys or the sweatshirt since that was confidential police information.

"Wow, that's a lot of bad stuff happening. Do the police

think the two incidents are related? Well, murder is hardly an incident, but you know what I mean."

"It's too soon to confirm, but we, they, think so. That's where we can use your help."

He placed his hand on his chest. "Me? What could I do?"

Josie said, "As we said before, Franny and Gloria had a huge fight in the driveway. It was around eleven when most people were in the back getting lunch. We're hoping you noticed who was still around and maybe even overheard what the fight was about."

The coffee pot gave up its final gurgle. I stood. "You think, and I'll pour."

I carried the pot and plate of muffins to the table. Josie slid a mug in front of her, adding a healthy dose of cream and a sprinkle of sugar. Russ added cream, his brows drawn together as he stirred.

"I can't believe Franny's dead and someone attacked Gloria. What's happening? Has the world stopped spinning correctly?"

I understood how Russ felt. However, my experience had been different, and bad things happened to good people. Most of the time, geography didn't significantly impact life altering events.

Josie said, "Yesterday was busy with lots of people coming and going."

He nodded. "Yeah, I was surprised how many folks turned up to clear the sidewalk of household items and help with demolition."

His words were slow, as if he were replaying events to get a clear picture of what we were trying to reconstruct.

"We finished up most of the demo by eleven. Chase, Seth, and Jacob were still filling a dumpster along with Erik Wool. Gordon had stopped with the party subs compliments of Renee and Sassy's Slices. I remember seeing Kelly Woods talking with Seth."

With a quick side glance at Josie, I said, "I didn't see Kelly. How long was she here?"

"I'm not sure. It was surprising she was chatting up Seth. I lost track of them when I went back into the apartment."

I rubbed my chin. "I never saw her. I wonder why she didn't say hello?"

Josie said, "Wait a second. She was looking at some glasses in that box by the fence."

"Right, that was around eleven. I got distracted when Franny and Gloria started yelling at each other. Gloria screamed, *how could you*? And Franny replied, *"It's not what you think."*

Josie said, "Sounds like a case of a classic misunderstanding."

I toyed with my mug. "Russ, what time did you see Kelly?"

"Maybe ten after eleven or later. I'm not sure. I didn't look at my watch, but I can say that Franny ran up to Chase and told him she was eating lunch and then going home. She'd had enough of Gloria for a lifetime."

"They were best friends," Josie said. "They wouldn't have stayed mad for long."

"Which was confirmed when Gloria said they talked and Franny invited her over."

Russ said, "You only have Gloria's word that's why she was going over. Did she say what happened when she arrived? Did they talk things out and clear the air?"

I shook my head. "We don't know. Gloria can't remember anything after she left her house. I'm sure it's from the trauma of her head injury. She may never remember." Drumming the tabletop, my mind raced with possibilities. Was the murderer already at Franny's before she spoke with Gloria? Is that something she'd recall? I pushed back from the table and grabbed a pad of paper and a pen from the junk drawer. I jotted down: was Franny alone during the call?

Josie said, "If Gloria doesn't remember driving over and we know she stopped to get ice cream, where could she have stopped? Maybe we should talk to whoever was working, see if they have security footage."

I made more notes. "What if Gloria didn't leave the store alone? She could have met up with a friend, dropped them off somewhere along the drive."

"Between Gloria's and Franny's, the only logical place to stop is the Quickie Mart. They sell ice cream," Russ said.

"I'm sure Casey's on top of this lead but you're right, we could stop over after dinner and see what we might learn. Who knows, maybe whoever was working last night will be there tonight," I added Quickie Mart to my notepad. "There's still the question of a new allergy since there was an EpiPen outside on the ground."

Josie said, "I'd like to know if it had been discharged."

"Russ, if there was a broken light at Franny's, how quickly would she have gotten it fixed?"

He sipped his coffee. "I know what you're thinking, and you're spot on. She maintained her house as if it were the White House. If anything had been broken, it would have been fixed immediately."

Which indicated to me the broken glass had occurred right before she'd been killed, and she didn't have time to clean it up, let alone replace the fixture. "Good to know."

"Who has a new allergy - Gloria?" he asked.

"No. We think Franny was newly diagnosed with something since there was medication at her place."

With a snap of his fingers he said, "Chase was worried about finding a bee nest in the exterior wall of the apartment yesterday. He's allergic and mentioned that if he got stung, we should use his EpiPen, apply ice to the sting, and get him to the hospital right away."

Josie tapped my computer keys. "According to a reputable medical site, if one sibling has an allergy, another sibling could also develop one. Bee allergies may be linked to heredity."

"We should assume Franny could have developed an allergy recently. I'll check with Casey to see if she found any additional EpiPens in Franny's car or her shoulder bag, even though I found a note that said call the doctor about more. That could indicate what was happening since, last I knew, she hadn't heard back from Franny's doctor."

I rubbed my chin. "There are so many open questions. Who was at Franny's before her death? What is the official cause of death? Did this person break the exterior light? The bathroom cabinets were ajar, was that a clue? Gloria's car is in Franny's garage with a bloody rag under it. How did Gloria end up at the river, injured?"

Josie said, "I'd like to know if Franny and Gloria talked in person last night. What if Gloria picked up the ice cream and was at Franny's along with the unknown person? For whatever reason, they decided to leave and were attacked. The unknown person could have taken Gloria to the river and dumped her, after which they killed Franny."

"I think somewhere in the middle is the truth."

Russ cleared his throat. "You think whoever killed Franny attacked Gloria and left her at the river, maybe hoping she'd die of her wound?"

"Or maybe even get swept downstream and drown." I gave him a somber look. "She doesn't recall if she was in the water at any point. Her clothes weren't wet, but she might have been in the water. If she had been washed downstream with the current, the injury or her death could have been explained by her going over the waterfalls and subsequent drowning. And don't forget we found fishing gear on the beach."

Josie gasped. "I never thought of that and the gear must have been staged."

I nodded.

Russ said, "I've seen Gloria fishing at the river before, and she always has her gear in the back of her Subaru; the only thing she'd need would be worms."

Now it made sense. The container of worms I found along the path going to the wormhole. "I'll bet she bought worms when she stopped at the Quickie Mart and planned to do a little night fishing. There was a headlamp near her fishing pole."

The pieces were beginning to fall into place. Too bad I wasn't sure what direction they were leading. "Hypothetically, she and Franny resolved their differences, and she was going fishing but was attacked before she left. Is that what we think happened?"

Josie nodded. "It makes sense. She's a potential witness to whoever killed Franny."

I picked up my phone. This was déjà vu.

Casey answered, "Butler."

"Casey, Temperance. Put a guard on Gloria when she leaves the hospital. If our hunch is correct, she knows who killed Franny and might have even been a witness to the entire thing. If she did, danger is just around the corner once the killer knows she's alive and well."

"I'm at the hospital waiting for her to be released. Are you sure?"

"Just like I was with Jonah. I'll explain everything when you get here, and if I'm wrong, it won't have caused any harm other than an officer spending a little time with Gloria and Chase."

"I'm on it. I should be by in a couple of hours."

"See you then." I set the phone aside and looked at Russ and Josie. "Does anyone want to take a drive to Gloria's with me before she gets home?"

8

———————

$\mathcal{I}$ rolled my SUV to a stop at the curb in front of Gloria's house. The street was deserted. If the police had been here, they were done investigating for now.

Josie peered out the passenger window. "How long before Chase brings Gloria home?"

"I'm guessing an hour, give or take."

Russ leaned through the front seats. "What are we looking for?"

Unbuckling my seatbelt, I pushed open the door. "I'm not sure. But I want to look around. Are you two coming?"

Both their doors opened, and in moments, they were flanking me. "We'll go around the garage side."

We moved in unison and I stole a glance at Russ. There was a determined gleam in his eyes as if he wanted to help solve the case but having him along for the drive wasn't the same thing as pulling him into the mystery.

"Keep your eyes peeled. You never know what we might find and Russ, if you see something, don't touch it. Just let me know." I hoped that didn't sound bossy but I knew Josie would tell me if she found a possible clue.

He nodded. "Got it. What do you think I could find?"

"The best I can say is anything that shouldn't be there."

We walked up the driveway and around the garage. Grass grew against the building; she hadn't planted any shrubs on this side of the house. It wasn't as tidy as Franny's home.

A small slate stone patio was off the back with an uncovered gas grill, a small wrought iron table with four chairs, and a deep blue umbrella. I smiled when I noticed a couple of flower pots with bright red geraniums pegged to each corner. The yard was surrounded by a six-foot-high stockade fence so the neighbors couldn't see into the space.

"Temperance, the sliding door is open." Josie pointed to the house. "Do you think we should go inside?"

"No, not without Gloria's permission. I want to check her fishing gear to see if there are empty spots but walking into her home isn't right."

"You're wondering if the gear at the river was hers?" Russ asked.

I nodded. "Correct. I'm assuming it was and she said yes. It's the logical answer but on the off-chance Gloria was mistaken, that could be a valuable detail."

"I can look through the side and back garage windows."

"Good idea. You do that and I'm going to circle the rest of the building."

Josie said, "I'm going to walk the fence line."

I smiled at her. She was beginning to think like an investigator and I wasn't sure if that was good or bad since it might put her in danger. "Be careful."

"Will do and you too."

We went in three separate directions. I continued to survey the base of the house and checked for more open windows. The only windows that were open were in the living room and there was a lamp on the table illuminating the room. Gloria must have forgotten to turn the light off when she left last night. I stepped around the hatchway, picked up the door and made a mental note to have someone lock it.

I circled back to Russ. He waited for me to get close when he said, "From the back window I can see her fishing gear. It's organized with items lining the shelves and a place to hang rods. There are empty spaces, so I'll conclude she had gear in her car."

But there wasn't. "Show me."

He cupped his hands around his eyes and leaned against the pane of glass. "Look to the right."

I scanned the space. Part of the garage looked like a hodgepodge of stuff - yard tools, paint cans, and rags. When I looked at the other side of the garage, it was the opposite. The bench and shelf unit were tidy with labels on the shelf, but I couldn't read them from this distance. For the rods, she had installed a vertical rack. It was out of direct sunlight, so it was a bit hard to see, but there were at least ten rods lined up, secured at the bottom and top. Fishing was a priority for Gloria.

"It's easy to see where her priorities lie." I heard Josie yell my name. The urgency in her voice propelled me into motion.

I raced to the back corner of the yard. "What's going on?"

She was standing several feet from the fence, looking up to a tree that leaned heavily to one side. "Gloria has a bee problem."

It took less than the blink of an eye to see the hordes of bees entering and exiting the hollow of an old maple tree. "Honey production." I grinned. "That would be good eating if there was a way to extract it safely."

"Yeah, that's not going to happen," Russ said.

Josie said, "I'll mention this to Gloria when we see her. They'll swarm before winter, but until then caution should be exercised."

I glanced over. "How do you know so much about bees and their habits?"

"I created a graphics campaign for an organization, Save the Bees. A little research made it easier to help with the event."

With a smile, I pointed to her forehead. "A font of knowledge is stored up there."

As we walked back to the SUV, I explained what Russ had found regarding fishing equipment.

"That makes sense. I knew she loved to be outdoors with a rod and reel whenever possible."

When we reached the sidewalk, I said, "Next we'll drive to Franny's and swing by the Quickie Mart on the way. I'd like to know if they have security cameras and get a visual to figure out if someone could have accosted Gloria there."

My cell pinged with an incoming text. "It's from Casey. Franny recently discovered she was allergic to bees and she'd been instructed on the importance of having an EpiPen close by at all times."

I spoke as I texted back. "Were her purse, car, and work checked for the devices?" The phone made a soft whoosh sound.

The little bubble appeared as Casey was texting me back. I read out loud, "Yes, we checked. The only place we found one was in her locker at the garden center."

Josie said, "That makes sense with all the plants and flowers the garden center would be bee heaven."

I smiled at her little pun. "And if we count the one on the ground outside her house, that makes two. She might not have had any more if she put one in her purse; it was usually with her."

"That's true," Josie said, "But if it were me, I'd have as many as the pharmacy would let me take home. I'd be scared to death, especially since she knew her brother was allergic and must have witnessed him getting stung at least once."

"If she's allergic to bees, would she also be allergic to honey?"

"It's possible but not necessarily." Russ said, "But if someone had introduced bees into her house, she could have been stung."

"I opened the kitchen window to let a bee out. Maybe this was just a simple tragedy. She got stung by a bee and couldn't find her medicine."

Russ frowned. "She didn't call for EMS."

My brow creased. "Where was her cell?" I pulled up the photos I had taken of the living room. I didn't see it on the sofa, chair, or table. "I'll text Casey to ask if she knows where Franny's phone is."

After sending the text, I walked to the SUV. "Ready to cruise to the Quickie Mart?"

Russ opened my door and closed it after I got in. From the corner of my eye, I could see Josie grin, thank heavens she was staring straight ahead so he couldn't see. I pinched her hand and she frowned as she rubbed it. Satisfied I made my point without having to say a word I eased the vehicle onto the street. As we drove away, a pick-up truck pulled into the driveway with two people in the cab. "I think Gloria and Chase are back."

"Should we go back and talk with them?" Josie asked.

I pulled a U-turn in the quiet street. "Yes. I want to see how she is and you can tell her about the bee hive at the back of her property line. Also, it would be good for Chase to know. Not that I think he'll go poking around back there but he's highly allergic."

I parked and we hurried across the grass. Josie pushed the doorbell, and we waited until Chase opened the door.

"Hello." He did a double-take as he looked from Josie, to Russ, to me. "I'm surprised to see you here."

"We wanted to see how Gloria was feeling. We stopped a minute ago and you weren't back yet. When I noticed the truck pull in the drive, I thought we'd come back for a quick check-in."

"Let me see if Gloria's up for company." He left the door open. I could hear him talking in a low voice to her. He returned. "She'd like you to come in." He pushed the door wider and swung open the screen.

We stepped inside. Gloria was sitting with her feet up in an overstuffed chair. She gave us a sad smile.

"Hi. It's good to see you ladies and Russ. Please sit down."

The three of us lined up, perched on the edge of the sofa.

Chase offered to get us drinks, but we declined. "We're only going to stay a minute," I said.

"Gloria, would you like something?"

"A diet soda please, with ice if it's not too much trouble."

He slipped from the room and she waited until he was gone. "I can't believe with all that Chase has going on he's willing to babysit me."

Josie said, "I'm sure he doesn't view it that way. You and Franny were best friends forever. It's probably his way of doing something his sister can't."

"I'm sure you're right but it's just awful. I can't believe she's gone." She rubbed her temples. "Thank you for helping find me this morning. I'm not sure if I'd still be here if you hadn't."

"Gloria, did you know that Franny was recently diagnosed with a bee allergy?" I asked.

"Yes. She got stung on her hand at work. Within minutes, her arm had swollen up like a plastic blowup doll. The venom was traveling up her arm and Kelly had to rush her to the emergency room. If it wasn't for Kelly's quick thinking, I shudder to think what might have happened." Her face fell. "I guess it bought Franny a few extra weeks of life. If I'd only known, we wouldn't have fought yesterday."

"It's easy to second guess actions after the fact, Gloria. Try not to dwell on it."

"Temperance, do you think the police will find out what happened to me?"

"I do."

"And I noticed my car wasn't in the driveway. Can you let them know it must have been stolen?"

I glanced at Russ and Josie. Should I tell her the car had been located at Franny's? It wasn't my place, even if I'd like to see her reaction. "Of course they'll find it. It's just a matter of time. Casey Butler is the lead on this case. You know she's tenacious."

She gave a slight nod, grimaced, and said, "I'm glad she's on the case. I couldn't do much better."

Chase returned with two glasses of soda, and he took a seat next to Gloria. "Is there any news on Gloria's attacker?"

"Nothing yet." I clasped my hands together. "Chase, can you think of anyone who would want to hurt your sister?"

He rubbed his chin. "Do I know of someone who would want to harm Franny? Absolutely no one. She was sweet to everyone. There wasn't a customer she couldn't charm at the garden center."

"Old or new boyfriends?" I asked.

"I don't think there's been anyone since Seth. He broke her heart and I'm not sure she was ready to date."

Gloria said, "Chase, she just started dating again but didn't tell me who. Franny said she didn't want to jinx it but she really liked the guy."

"News to me." He frowned and sipped his soda.

"Do you know who might have stopped by her place last night, before Gloria was supposed to arrive?"

"She called and said Gordon was there. He brought over a box of cupcakes for the girls. I knew about the argument between her and Gloria and I wasn't surprised to hear that they were going to get together over chocolate and talk things out."

"It was our usual way. Franny and I didn't argue often but we always made up over sweets."

"Gloria," I said, "Do you remember anything more after pulling out of your driveway? You mentioned something about picking up ice cream. Did you take it from your freezer, or did you stop and buy it?"

Josie was watching me as I watched Gloria.

"I've been thinking about that since we talked at the river and I noticed my fishing gear was in the sand. I remember thinking I needed to stop and get some night crawlers in case I wanted to go fishing in the morning. The Quickie Mart has decent worms, and I usually get pints of ice cream from them since they carry the SoCo brand we like." Tears welled up in her eyes. "Liked."

I leaned closer. "You were going to fish this morning, but what about last night?"

She smiled at me for the first time since yesterday. "You don't fish, do you?"

With a shake of my head, I said, "Sorry. No. Did I say something wrong?"

"For night fishing, I'd need my headlamp and brightly colored or luminous lures. Worms would never be the bait I'd use. Before you ask, there aren't a lot of people around here who like to fish at night. The mosquitoes are brutal, and now that you've made your way down the bank to our fishing holes, you know navigating that in the dark would be tricky."

Chase said, "I never saw the appeal of night fishing."

Josie asked, "Did Franny ever go with you?"

"Sometimes I could convince her. Mostly, I went alone. I love every aspect of fishing."

"Gloria, I don't want you to think I'm invading your privacy, but what did you and Franny argue about at my place yesterday?"

"It doesn't matter anymore. She's gone and I have to live

with the fact that we fought over something that happened so long ago it didn't even matter anymore."

Chase took her hand. "If Temperance thinks it might help figure out what happened, I think you should tell her."

She tipped her head and stared at him. "You have no idea what you're asking me to do. Last night when we talked, Franny and I agreed never to discuss it again."

"Was that when you were at her place or on the phone?" Josie asked.

"I was sitting in the armchair in her living room and we agreed to never, ever…" The color drained from her face. "I *did* see her last night before she died."

I withdrew my cell to call Casey. "You're starting to remember, Gloria. Which means you and Chase need to be vigilant. Whoever attacked you might not be thrilled you didn't drift downstream. You probably saw or heard something you weren't supposed to."

9

Gloria sat in stunned silence. She wasn't talking or moving. Chase held her hand, murmuring soothing words while we waited for Casey to arrive.

The sound of a car door slamming drifted through the front door. I stood and walked outside. "Casey, thanks for getting here so quickly. Gloria is starting to remember. In conversation, she mentioned whatever the girls were fighting about, they agreed never to discuss it again, and it wasn't when they were on the phone. She remembers being in Franny's living room."

"I stopped at the station to check on security for her and got here as fast as I could after we hung up. They should be here shortly." Casey closed her eyes briefly. "Her attack is directly related to Franny's death."

"That's pretty much confirmed now." I glanced at the house. "We should go in. Gloria's been silent since she realized there could be an additional threat to her life."

"Understandable. Did she say anything else?"

"Only that you don't fish at night with worms."

Her eyes widened briefly as the significance sank in. "Good job, Temperance."

I waited while she called the police station and checked on the protection detail. With a traffic light on her street, anyone trying to approach the house would be obvious.

A muddy blue hatchback slowly drove by. The driver had a ball cap pulled low on their head, and when they saw me they accelerated and zipped down the street.

"Protection detail will be here within the half-hour," Casey said as we walked to the house.

"Before we go in do you want to see something awesome and scary at the same time?" I asked.

She shot me a side glance. "Related to the case?"

"Not really. We found it when we were looking around before Gloria arrived," I didn't specifically say we were snooping, but Casey would read through the subtext, "Josie looked around the back yard."

"You've piqued my interest. Show me."

I pointed to the side yard and we headed that way.

"Did you happen to discover anything else while you were," she coughed, "waiting?"

"Russ looked in the garage windows, and fishing gear seemed to be missing. Gloria confirmed it was her stuff on the beach but there was nothing in her car."

"That's good to know."

"And she doesn't remember where her car is - she asked if you were looking for it."

Casey nodded. "We have to finish processing it for evidence. I still can't figure out how the car was in the garage with blood inside it. The blood drops on the concrete, I can surmise, came from when they moved Gloria from the car and transported her to the river."

"That would mean that whatever vehicle was used will have her blood inside."

Casey's lips thinned. "Or not. If they put a tarp or even a shower curtain down, they could have tossed that almost anywhere."

She had a point. Whoever did this had time to dump Gloria and drive almost anywhere to get rid of additional evidence. That is, if they realized it. How many crime shows or books have they watched or read?

When we reached the tree line, I pointed to the maple tree with the buzz of bees. "Look at the activity. Can you imagine the honey that must be building up in there?"

"It makes me think of Winnie the Pooh and the honey tree. Where Pooh is trying to figure out a way to extract a snack."

I chuckled. "I'm not going to pretend I'm a rain cloud, but it got me thinking. I found a bee in Franny's kitchen. Do you think it was simply an accident and she might have gotten stung? If she died from anaphylaxis?"

She gave me an assessing look. "Then why didn't she inject herself with the Epinephrine?"

"It looks like the place was searched. Maybe she forgot where she put it?" My answer was weak, but it was all I could come up with. "Did you find her cell phone?"

"Yes, it was in the console of the work SUV."

"Huh." I turned away from the hive. "I'm sure Gloria is concerned we're not inside yet. We should go."

Thoughts tumbled over in my brain. Josie and Russ still didn't put anyone new around my house at the time of the argument. Maybe Gloria could.

I pulled open the screen. Casey went into the living room first.

She nodded to Josie and Russ. "Gloria, I'm sure it's good to be home."

"It is. Did Temperance tell you that I was at Franny's last night? I know we talked. I still can't remember if we cleared the air completely, but I'd like to think so. It wouldn't be right for her to pass with us being mad at each other." She dissolved into tears. "She's my best friend."

"I'm sure in time you'll remember everything, and it will

give you comfort. If you know that you talked about your argument, you must have agreed to put it behind you."

She sniffed and nodded. "You're right."

Casey pulled up a straight-back chair and sat down to be eye-level with Gloria. "Yesterday, at Temperance's house when you and Franny argued, do you remember who was around and might have overheard you?"

Gloria frowned. Chase held tight to her hand. Josie and Russ sat up straighter. We were all waiting for the big reveal. Would we be disappointed?

"Let me think." She closed her eyes as the digital wall clock flipped numbers in what seemed like slow motion. "It was late morning, and Franny had been talking about the fire that could have destroyed Temperance's house like it had the bakery. The guys - Erik, Chase, and Jacob - were filling the dumpster. Gordon was looking through what was left on the sidewalk. Kelly Woods stopped by to talk to Seth. I remember seeing Russ walking from the street to the garage with a clipboard in his hand, and of course Temperance and Josie were there. They had just brought Hank back from the nature preserve."

That was a very clear picture, and basically she had just named every possible suspect.

"Could any of those people have overheard your fight?" Casey asked.

"Temperance and Josie went inside, and Russ was writing something on a clipboard as he hurried by, so they wouldn't have heard anything."

"What about Kelly and Seth? Were they close enough?"

She closed her eyes again. "They could have overheard us as well as Gordon. Chase and Jacob were going in and out of the back apartment, so I don't think they did." She looked at Chase. "Did you know what we argued about?"

"I didn't overhear the argument, but Franny told me later in the day."

Her voice dropped to a whisper. "Oh."

He said, "Gloria, you need to tell the police what you and Franny were talking about. It might be relevant to her death since it involves unresolved issues in town."

"Chase, I promised her never to talk about it. Ever."

"That was before she died. It can't upset her now, and if that same someone is responsible for her death *and* your brush with mortality, they must be held responsible."

"I don't know." She chewed her lower lip, her gaze wouldn't meet Casey's. "Can I think about it?"

"How about if we leave?" I suggested it to Josie and Russ. "You can speak with Casey privately."

She nodded. "That might be better." With a glance at Casey she asked, "Can we keep this just between us?"

"I'm sorry, but that's not possible. If it's relevant to why Franny died and your attack it must be on the official police report."

It was kind that Casey hadn't used the words killed or murdered to Gloria and Chase. She was on edge and he had lost his sister to a senseless death.

"Casey, we're headed back to my place."

She nodded. "Sounds good. We'll talk later."

Russ, Josie, and I left the house. The sound of tires squealing caught my attention. I couldn't see the car that made them, but it left an uneasy feeling in the pit of my gut. "I'll be right back. I need to tell Casey something."

Josie said, "We'll wait in the car."

I jogged to the house, tapped on the door jamb and called out, "Casey, a word, please?" I waited about ten feet from the house. I didn't want Gloria or Chase to overhear us.

She crossed the grass and, with her back to the house, said, "What's up?"

"Earlier, when you were on the phone, a blue car cruised by really slowly. I couldn't tell who the driver was; they had a hat pulled down low over their face, and just now when we came out I heard the chirp of tires on the pavement. I didn't see the car but I have a gut feeling someone is watching this house."

Casey strode from the sidewalk to the center of the road and scanned up and down the street. "It's all quiet now, which doesn't mean you're wrong, it just means no one is currently lingering. I'll pass this information on to the officer when she arrives."

"Good. I'm not sure if it matters, but I thought I'd let you know."

"Temperance, I never dismiss your observations. Now, not to be rude, but I can't share with you whatever Gloria is about to tell me if Russ is around. It's stretching it with you and Josie, but since I'm relying on your help to solve this case as special friends of the department, I'll tell you what I can."

"Understood." I didn't feel the need to explain why Russ was with us now or justify that he was the one who discovered the fishing equipment was missing. I had already told her that, so she knew his input had helped.

"I'll see you later." Casey walked to the front door with her spine straight, determined to get to the truth no matter where it might lead.

This time when I pulled away from the curb I didn't look back. "I'm still going to drive by the Quickie Mart to check out the cameras. Russ, if you'd go in and see if you notice a monitor where the person on the register might see the gas pumps and other areas that would be helpful. Josie and I can stroll to scope out the rest of the area."

Josie said, "I thought we were going home?"

I flashed her a grin. "We're taking the scenic route. If we discover interesting facts that help Casey and the police close the case, then it's worth the extra few minutes."

She settled into the passenger seat. "I've got time."

Russ leaned forward. "Me too."

I stopped at the gas pump and got out. Russ got out too and said, "I'm going to get some bait."

Josie closed the passenger door and stretched her arms over her head. "Grab some ice cream too."

Clever girl - getting Russ to retrace Gloria's steps was another good idea and he'd keep his eyes peeled for monitors while inside. I looked up and saw cameras positioned at the corners of the store, facing the parking area. After I inserted my credit card into the machine, I fit the gasoline nozzle in the SUV while I scanned the area. There were cameras overlooking each pump.

Josie strolled over. "I'm going to stretch my legs."

I nodded. "Keep your eyes peeled."

We didn't know if Gloria had also filled up on gas, so she might have parked along the side of the building. I finished filling the tank and took my receipt. Josie came back to the car as Russ exited the store.

He said, "I got three pints; maple walnut, chocolate peppermint, and caramel fudge." He closed the door. "There are monitors all over the place with the screens rotating to the pumps, the store, and around the perimeter. I can't see how anyone can be accosted here. Oh, and Keith was working last night and he'll be back tonight at five."

"Good to know." I was a little disappointed we hadn't found out more. Later when I went back to talk with Keith I might get more details such as whether he remembered anyone approaching Gloria.

"Does this mean whoever attacked Gloria didn't meet up with her here?" Russ asked.

"It's too soon to rule out any possibilities." I took the direct route to Franny's thinking that's what Gloria would have done too. It took less than ten minutes. "From the time we left Gloria's, stopped at the convenience store, and drove here it was eighteen minutes."

"Why is that important?" Josie asked.

"If they talked on the phone and agreed to get together, whoever is responsible had time to show up at Franny's and get ready to execute their plan."

Russ said, "It was planned, not a reaction to a stressful situation? That makes it premeditated?"

"Obviously I don't know for sure but yes, it's possible the plan was to take Franny out of the equation. Whatever the girls argued about has been a secret for a long time and recent events, AKA my fire, brought up something." I tapped a finger on the steering wheel. "Josie, how many unsolved fires have happened in town that you can recall?"

"Time frame?"

"Fifteen years, give or take." I calculated the girls' ages and based my time frame on what they may have witnessed as teenagers.

"Russ, do you remember? Other than the abandoned house outside of town, the greenhouse at Twigs and Petals."

He said, "There was a barn fire too at the Nardin's farm. No people or livestock were injured, it was just the hay barn. They attributed that to lightning but we didn't have any severe storms in the area that night."

"Nardin, as in Gordon, the pizza delivery guy? And Gloria?"

"One and the same," Russ said.

Josie said, "It was their grandparents' place. He and Gloria are second cousins or something. Everyone in town got together and we held an old-fashioned barn raising like they did back in the day. It was fun but a lot of hard work."

"Don't you find it interesting that two unsolved fires, the barn and greenhouse, and the people who were affected by them were near Gloria and Franny when they argued? I might be taking a leap here since Gloria said my fire ignited old feelings. What if they knew who was responsible for either or both of those fires, and it's a secret they've kept for years?"

Josie said, "Maybe Franny was wracked with guilt and wanted to confess."

Russ shook his head. "I can't believe those girls are responsible for arson."

I pulled into my drive, shut the vehicle off and turned in my seat. "What if they knew who did it and either Franny or Gloria wanted to tell the police what they knew or to try and convince the guilty party to come forward?"

Josie gave a low whistle and Russ shook his head.

My shoulders slumped. "That *is* motive to keep someone quiet permanently."

---

10

*R*uss had left. Josie and I were spooning ice cream directly from the pint containers into our mouths. Hank was curled up on the small cushion next to my porch chair, his gentle snores soothing.

Josie looked at me over the pint, "What's your instinct telling you?"

I paused with the spoon midway to my mouth. "Other than the two cases are connected and someone overheard the argument about whatever it was in the past that the ladies felt they had to keep a secret until the grave?"

She nodded. "That about sums it up."

"There's so much we don't know. It's hard to say. We need to know how Franny died. We need to know how the EpiPen ended up outside. We need the security footage from the Quickie Mart. We need to know if Gloria bought bait. The most important tidbit, we need to know who else was at Franny's when Gloria arrived."

Her lips tipped. "That's a lot of *'we need to know'*."

"Once we have those details, the case is solved and the guilty person arrested." I frowned. "Why do you think Kelly would need to speak with Seth? To come over here to talk with him, do you think that's odd?"

"Do you know what I think is even more odd? Last night, there was a break-in at Twigs and Petals."

"Right, I forgot about that. We can ask Casey about that when she gets here. If she can share the specifics with us, that is."

She asked, "Doesn't it feel like eons ago that you had people running around here, emptying the apartment, doing demo, and getting ready for reconstruction tomorrow?"

"It's surreal. Through it all, Russ and you have been a tower of strength." I stuck the spoon in the ice cream. "What I'm struggling with is that the bakery fire was the catalyst. It's not like I broke a mirror, walked under a ladder or had a black cat cross my path. Maybe moving to Oak Hollow wasn't the best idea."

"Long-buried secrets have a way of coming out eventually." She stood. "I'm putting my pint in the freezer. Are you done?"

I handed it to her. "Thanks"

The screen door banged after her, and I thought about the broken light fixture outside Franny's house. Was it related to the events that occurred last night? I closed my eyes and tipped my head back. Hank gave a sharp bark and nuzzled my leg. I picked him up and he settled into my lap. I closed my eyes again and replayed the scene at Franny's. I heard Josie come back to the porch and settle in her chair.

She waited several minutes. "Any clarity?"

"No. I can't even think of anything to research, except…" I looked over and she held my laptop in her hands.

"The greenhouse fire?" She passed it to me. "You're right. That has to be the connection."

"Or the Nardin barn fire. Do you remember when they happened?"

She tapped her lips with her index finger. "They both

happened around the same time I think. The barn was in the summer, before the first haying. I thought it was weird when someone mentioned that it was a good thing."

"If it had been full, the livestock would have lost feed for the winter months. It was a working farm, correct?"

"Yes they had cows, chickens, and a huge garden with a farm stand selling vegetables right up until Halloween, with the best pumpkins. Gordon used to help out at the stand; he was a good salesperson."

"And the greenhouse fire?" I knew I could look up the details, but Josie's impressions might be valuable in a different way, from a local person's perspective.

"I think it was the following spring, like early, maybe March? It was bad; the fire destroyed the entire greenhouse. At least the fire department arrived quickly before the flames could spread. That might have ended Twigs and Petals."

I flipped open the laptop and typed in the sparse details and scanned the results. "Okay, so the greenhouse fire was in March. It says here the final report labeled it as suspicious but without a clear cause." I looked up. "Was the investigation bungled?"

She shrugged. "I'm not sure. I was in college at the time so I don't really remember much talk about it."

"Yeah, it wouldn't have hit your radar." I made a mental note to ask Casey about it and the barn fire. She could access details that weren't readily available to the public.

"What time do you think Casey will get here?"

"Anytime now." I searched for the barn fire. "Was arson suspected at the Nardin's?"

"I have no idea. I wasn't friends with Gordon in school. He was behind me by a couple of years." She looked at me. "What are you thinking?"

"There is no such thing as a coincidence."

With a low whistle, she said, "If you believe that's true

then everything that's happened in the last twenty-four plus hours is connected?"

Nodding slowly I said, "Yes. The girls argued about some long-ago secret. What if they were fighting about the barn or greenhouse fires? Kelly just happened to stop by to talk to Seth. Gordon, the grandson of the family who had a fire and Gloria's cousin is also close by. One of them overheard the girls and was upset."

Her eyes grew round as saucers. "Your suspects are Kelly, Seth, and Gordon?"

"Who do you think attacked Franny and Gloria?" I hated that it sounded like a challenge, but my hope was it'd make her have a gut reaction and blurt out her first thought.

She pulled her lips tight and shook her head. "I don't know."

"You have some ideas." I sat up and turned my chair around. Hank gave me the doxie side look, as if I shouldn't be disturbing his nap. I ran my hand down the length of his silky back, and he closed his eyes again.

Her chin dipped. "Temperance, do you know how hard this is? To be sitting here knowing there are bad people in my hometown?"

Softening my voice, I said, "They're not bad people, they're just doing bad things. That's the difference."

I waited for Josie to understand. This was difficult for her; she'd known these people her entire life. Being a newcomer, they didn't mean as much to me. I felt awful that people were struggling with such profound feelings that they resorted to violence, but I had a different perspective. My experience had taught me it could happen anywhere, in big cities or small towns.

Her words were halting as she said, "It's like a sharp thrust of pain to my gut. I think you're right. They're the most logical. At first, I thought it was Gloria, but there's no way she could have hurt herself, left her car at Franny's, and been dumped at the river." She swatted a fly away.

That's what was bugging me. The river. "Did Gloria have any insect bites on her?"

Josie's face scrunched up. "Like mosquitos? I'm not sure. Why?"

The sound of a vehicle slowing drew my attention. I stood, holding Hank in my arms, and crossed to the railing. "Casey's here."

She lifted her hand, acknowledging me before she got out of her truck. Hank perked up and gave two quick happy barks as if he recognized our friend.

Taking the porch steps two at a time she said, "Hey guys. Sorry it took me so long to get here."

Hank wriggled to get down and he raced over to her the moment his feet hit the decking.

"Hello Hank, are you happy to see me?" She scratched his ears and he rolled over on his back, exposing his belly for a rub. Casey obliged.

"How have you two been? It's been an eventful day."

"You aren't justa kidding." My granddad's old-fashioned saying slipped out. "How are you? Tired? Would you like coffee or something stronger?"

"Water, please. I'm parched." She flopped onto the porch swing.

"Josie?"

She said, "Please."

I went inside to get three glasses and a bowl of water. I kept thinking about bug bites. Shouldn't Gloria have been loaded with them after being that close to the water overnight?

I put the glasses and bowl for Hank on a tray and walked backside first through the screen door. "Here you go."

Josie took the bowl and placed it next to Hank's bed.

Casey watched me sit and sip my water. "What's bothering you?"

"Other than murder and an injured woman?"

"Well that, but something's buzzing around your brain. Out with it."

Josie looked from me to Casey and back again. "Temperance's brain has been in overdrive, but she's keeping her thoughts close. I think she was waiting for you to get here."

Casey spread her hands wide and leaned back on the swing. "I'm here. Talk."

"How's Gloria?" It was best to start with an open-ended question. As a police officer, she'd know exactly what I was doing and she'd give me just enough information to keep me asking questions until I said what was on my mind.

"As well as can be expected. She's got a whopper of a headache, and Chase plans on sleeping on the sofa tonight to keep an eye on her."

"It's good that she won't be alone. Has she regained more of her memory?"

"Spits and spurts. You know how amnesia can be with a trauma victim."

I nodded. "Any chance she's faking it?"

Casey leaned forward, her elbows propped on her knees. "Why would you think that's a possibility?"

Before I answered, I asked, "Does she have any bug bites?"

"I don't know. I never thought to ask or look." She gave me a knowing smile. "I know where you're headed now."

Josie asked, "Oh. I get it, I think. Can you call the emergency room and ask a nurse if she had any?"

"That I can do." She tapped a few times on the screen and put the phone to her ear. "Allison, hello this is Officer Butler. I was in the emergency room earlier this morning with Gloria Nardin. I was hoping you could tell me if her insect bites were severe or if you'd even taken note of them." She nodded. "Sure, I'll hold."

I snapped my fingers. "How are she and Gordon related again?"

Josie said, "Maybe second cousins, I'm not sure." Color slipped from her face. "Another connection to the barn."

"Like cogs on a wheel, my friend."

Casey held up her finger. "You're sure?" She tipped her head to the side. "Thanks. I appreciate the information. Bye."

She set the phone on the small side table. "Gloria had ant and mosquito bites on her arms, hands and lower legs and feet as well as her head and neck."

"There goes that theory." I looked across to the nature preserve.

"Which was?" Josie asked.

"Gloria didn't go to the river under her own steam. If she did, pretending to be more seriously hurt than she was, she would have thought to put on insect repellent. As an avid fisherwoman, she'd know how nasty the bugs were next to the water's edge at night." I was done beating around the bush. "Casey, what was the argument about between Gloria and Franny?" My gut clenched. I was sure it was about one of the fires from years ago. They knew something, maybe even who started them and kept the secret for too many years.

"Gloria said my bakery fire brought up old feelings and bad memories. But it was more than just emotions. Did they know who started the fire? Is that what they argued about yesterday morning, when almost anyone could have overheard them?"

Casey clasped her hands in her lap. She looked between me and Josie. "This goes without saying, but what we talk about on this porch is confidential."

I arched my brow.

She said, "I know it is, but it makes me feel better to say the actual words."

Josie's words came out in a rush. "I can leave if you want. Not that I'd ever breathe a word of this to anyone."

"I trust you two. Like I said, it's a tick box for me to remind you both."

Her head bobbed and I said, "Casey, we've got tight lips. No one will hear a peep from us."

"Fires." Just one word came from her lips.

"The greenhouse and barn fires were the work of a single person?" I asked.

"From what Gloria said, yes. Now we only have her word but she said that Franny was responsible for both of them."

Josie gasped. "That's not possible."

Casey arched a brow. "Why not? Other than she's not alive to defend herself?"

"She was afraid of fire, any kind, even a candle. When we were in the holiday choir for the pageant, she cried when they said we had to carry candles. It was only a battery-operated candle, but until the choir director passed them out and she saw it with her own eyes, she sobbed."

I said, "People get over childhood fears."

She shook her head. "Nope. Not Franny. She wouldn't even have a lit candle at her table in a restaurant. That's how scared she was. To say she started the fires is covering up the truth. Gloria knows who started them, and pinning it on Franny is an easy way to close those cases forever."

Josie had a point. There was no way to disprove that Franny wasn't involved. "Was Chase in the room when Gloria told you this information?"

"No. I'd asked him to leave the room due to the ongoing police investigation. The less sensitive information that gets out, the better."

"Alright, so who knows the argument was about the fires, plural? Either Kelly, Gordon, or Seth could have overheard, and one of them is responsible. Kelly got insurance money to rebuild. Gordon is Gloria's cousin so he's at the bottom of the list now and Seth, well I don't know how he plays into any of this. We need to ask Kelly why she had to speak with him yesterday."

"I already did that when I stopped at the garden center to take her statement about the break-in last night."

I had forgotten about that detail. "Is that connected to these four cases?"

"You mean the two arson cases, the attack on Gloria, and Franny's death?" She smiled. "Temperance, if you ever want to join the police force as a special detective, I'll put in a good word for you with the boss."

"No, thank you. I'm looking forward to baking again. Not being an active part of the force."

Josie said, "I don't know Tee, you've got a mind for murder."

"Just cupcakes with a side of murder," I said.

11

———————

*C*asey asked, "Any chance you've got cupcakes in the house? I haven't eaten since breakfast, and some sugar will help tide me over to dinner. Especially if you want the details about Twigs and Petals."

I stood and grinned. "Bribery, Officer Butler?"

"Maybe we should think of it as supporting your local police department, your civic duty."

I laughed. "Come on in and fix yourself a plate of leftovers. I've got plenty to choose from. Josie, you too. It's been a long day and you must be hungry." What I wanted was to get us off the porch while we talked about the multiple cases.

Hank trotted in as soon as I opened the door, and the ladies were right behind him. Josie stacked plates and silverware on the counter. I withdrew leftover pizza and a bowl of Pasta Bolognese from the refrigerator, along with salad fixings. On the counter under the glass dome were six vanilla frosted lemon cupcakes.

Casey said, "Those look amazing. Why didn't you put the lemon ones out yesterday?"

"I made a dozen to add a little variety since not everyone likes chocolate and a four-legged baby, who shall remain

89

nameless (Hank) decided to take a bite out of six. I frosted the survivors and here we are. Cupcakes for us."

She chuckled. "At least they didn't make him sick."

"He has an iron stomach." I rubbed his velvety ears.

Josie put a filled plate in the microwave.

Giving Casey a casual glance, even though I was dying to know what happened I asked, "How long are you going to keep us in suspense about Twigs & Petals?"

She sat at the table. "The entire situation is strange."

"What isn't about this case?" Josie said.

"The main part of the store where the cash registers and office area are located has security cameras on twenty-four seven. The greenhouses have cameras that switch views. If someone knew the schedule, they could easily slip past them. I pointed out to Kelly that she should change and make them all active at all times."

"Did something happen to one of the other buildings?"

The microwave beeped and Josie withdrew her plate and put Casey's in.

"Yes. There's an office with computers and an equipment garage with rototillers, tractors, chainsaws, and the like that's used for the landscaping side of the business."

"Where Chase and Gloria work?" I asked.

"Correct. Kelly received a notification of a disturbance, but she was on a date and didn't get it until later. She called it in at about eleven, but the break-in occurred around nine o'clock."

"Did she say what was taken or destroyed?"

Josie glanced at me. "There must be expensive equipment that would be easy to grow legs and walk out of there."

Casey nodded. "Interesting way of putting it, but you're correct, there is a lot to steal. The chainsaws alone are worth a pretty penny. However, Kelly doesn't think anything was taken. She can't be sure about things like shovels, pitchforks and other smaller items but the expensive items are all accounted for."

Pursing my lips, my mind raced with what we knew about the cases. "Then why do you think they're connected?"

"The medical examiner believes Franny died around ten."

Those words dangled in the air.

"Cause?" I leaned against the counter as the microwave beeped again. I handed Casey her plate. "Does he know what she died from?"

"Anaphylaxis. But he hasn't found the area where Franny was stung."

"She doesn't have any welts on her body?"

"No, and before you ask he's sure bee venom was the cause of death. We should have more information in a few days."

Josie asked, "How can he be certain?"

"I didn't want the nitty gritty details about tissues and such. I took him at his word." She bit into her pizza.

I admired how nothing fazed her except for being told about the specific details of a death. Then she was a little squeamish. "So we'll work forward from there. Let's get back to Gloria. She came right out and said Franny was responsible for the fires. She must not realize that other people know about her fear of fire."

Josie said, "I know what I saw. The first time was long before the barn fire. We might have been eight or ten years old."

"Did Gloria say anything more about last night? Does she remember being at Franny's?"

"She said no. But there was something in her eye, and the way her gaze focused on the front window. My gut is telling me she knows more than she's saying and is scared."

I nodded, agreeing with that assessment. I felt that way from the beginning, even if she did have a head wound, things didn't add up.

"With so little to go on, are you up for brainstorming the situation?"

Casey arched one eyebrow. "Have we compiled enough data?"

I lifted a shoulder. "Who knows? But I'd like to try."

Josie said, "I'm with Temperance on this. We should at least try to assemble the puzzle pieces - at least the outline. It's the best way to solve it. At least that's how it worked a week ago."

I stood and paced the perimeter of the kitchen. There were times I thought better on my feet. "We don't know enough about the barn and greenhouse fires from ten years ago. Casey, can you pull the files and see what you can uncover? Were there similarities in the ignition source and how long they had potentially been burning before the fire department was called?" I snapped my fingers, "We shouldn't overlook the abandoned house either. Was that before the barn or some point after?"

"Copy that. Good point on the third fire. It might be unrelated but we should determine the status."

"We'll fast forward on the assumption that the ladies knew who started the fires and why."

Josie said, "I would agree with that statement. Another data point, we know Franny was triggered by the fire at the Early Rise."

Casey placed her fork on the plate. "Which makes me wonder, why does the truth need to come out now? The guilty party was arrested for the bakery fire and we know the reason behind it."

I nodded. "It was due to pettiness and jealousy."

"And control," Josie tossed out.

"True. After all these years of Franny keeping quiet, other than the fire last week bringing up bad memories, why now?" I knew that question had been asked, but I felt it was worth repeating.

"Maybe she had a falling out with the person who started the blazes."

Casey said, "You're assuming it's one person. There could be two or more people involved."

"Could it have been Gloria?" I asked. Answering myself, I said, "Not likely given that her family's farm was one of the casualties. Also not out of the question, she could have been protecting her accomplice."

"Fast forward to yesterday." Josie said, "We know who was around when the ladies melted down. However, I don't remember seeing anyone react or try to interject to deescalate the situation."

I agreed. "Chase and Jacob should be on the suspect list. I know we tried to narrow it down to Kelly, Seth, and Gordon, but he's dropped down too, since it was his grandparents' farm. It would more likely be one of the others."

Casey waved her forkful of pasta in the air. "Not impossible. Family dynamics can be difficult and unpredictable."

"Which could tie to Gloria trying to protect someone. Do we agree there are five decent suspects?"

Josie said, "Kelly is at the top of my list. Not only did she lose a greenhouse, but her business was broken into again. Events seem more of a nuisance than a problem, but just the same. Franny would have let her into the house and Gloria wouldn't have been concerned if she were at the house since they work for her."

Josie scraped her plate into the trash can and set it in the sink before putting the cake stand in the middle of the table. "I wouldn't be afraid of her either."

"When I spoke with Hattie and Babette, they mentioned Franny had a lot of visitors last night, but never said who. Is it possible the exterior light was smashed to prevent the neighbor ladies from knowing who had stopped over?"

"Kelly says she was on a date but wouldn't say who it was with. And the light being smashed is a logical assumption but," Casey said, "did it happen before or after Franny died?"

I thought of the EpiPen lying on the ground. "Here's a horrible thought. Our killer knew Franny needed the pen, and the bathroom had been searched. Could the killer have volunteered to get the medicine, found it in the bathroom, and then deliberately withheld it from Franny?"

Casey gave a thoughtful nod, "Very possible. It was full."

There was a sob in Josie's voice. "I can't believe anyone would be that cruel."

"It's awful to think about, let alone say, but we need to look at all possibilities. If Gloria wasn't involved, she witnessed the events, and when she tried to get away, she was attacked and left at the river."

Casey asked, "How likely do you think it is that she's not involved?"

"Honestly, I'm at a fifty-fifty split. She knows more than she's saying, and I'm sure a lot of that is for Chase's benefit. They've been friends for years and they work together."

Josie cleared her throat. "Um, well, they're more than friends. They've dated on and off for years. He wants to get married; but she's not ready to commit."

Casey perked up. "That's very interesting. Now I under-stand why he wanted to be with her at the hospital despite his loss and why he's staying with her."

"But it doesn't explain why she had to talk with you after he left the room. What secret is Gloria keeping from Chase that would be so horrible she didn't want him to know?"

"Unless it was true that Franny committed arson," Josie said. "If it were me, I'd want to protect the man I loved."

"Maybe she did," Casey said.

"Interesting. If she did, then who knocked her out?"

"Franny's accomplice."

Josie shook her head and knocked over her glass, spilling

water across the table. She threw a wad of napkins on it and, without looking up, asked, "Why leave her at the water? Wouldn't it have been just as convincing to leave her unconscious at Franny's?"

I took the wad of wet napkins and tossed them in the trash. Josie was spiraling, and I needed her to have a clear head to answer questions about our other suspects.

"Josie, take a breath." I gently guided her to the chair. "Let's table the Gloria topic. Tell me about Seth Armstrong. Is he friends with everyone?"

She exhaled. "Yes. Seth, Chase, and Jacob played sports together. They were referred to as the three musketeers. If you saw one the other two weren't far behind. Like I said earlier Seth dated Franny but I heard they broke up months ago."

"It's not like that now?" Casey asked.

Josie scrunched up her face. "Not really. It might be that adulting has gotten in the way. They don't spend much time together. I was surprised to see Seth show up."

"He's a sales rep?"

"Pharmaceuticals. He wanted to be a doctor but didn't pass the MCAT after college. Instead, he went the pharmaceutical route."

I asked, "If he doesn't work for Kelly, why would she have come over here to speak with him?"

"That's one question on my mind," Casey said.

Josie looked between us. "They could be dating?"

"What?" That was quite a shock. "I thought Kelly had a long-term boyfriend. When Casey mentioned she was on a date, I figured that's who she was with."

"No, she had a boyfriend for years. From the OH grapevine, I heard she dumped him eight months ago."

"Always a reliable source," Casey frowned. "Did you go to school together?"

"No. She's four years older than me. She took over her

family's business after graduating from business school. Plants were second nature to her since she grew up at the garden center."

"Her family owned it when the greenhouse burned?" Casey asked.

"Yes. The Woods family started the business in the 1950's."

Casey nodded. "Good to know details other than from the owners. Has the business thrived?"

"I assume so. Kelly's expanded into landscaping and added a holiday shop that's open from fall until January."

Drumming her fingertips on the table, Casey looked out the side window but she wasn't taking in the view of the bird-feeder. "I need to check into the fire. There was an insurance settlement."

"Are you wondering if Kelly was looking for another 'problem'?" I added the air quotes to problem to add the extra zing in my meaning. "Like could the break-in have led to another insurance claim?"

"If she has cash flow problems, it's a possibility. There's no way to know until I dig."

That wasn't information that would be available to me even if I dug into it. "Could Seth have been the burglar? Maybe they set it up yesterday."

"Aren't we getting off the topic of Franny's death?" Josie asked.

I could hear the anguish-tinged words, and my heart constricted. Her old schoolmate had died, and another was attacked. If the incidents were related, we'd figure it out. It didn't have to be right now. "How about we enjoy the cupcakes and stop talking about the case?"

She brightened. "I know, you should give Casey a mini tour of your new space." Smiling at Casey, she continued, "Wait until Temperance describes it to you. It'll spring to life.

I can almost smell the mouthwatering aroma of cookies, or bread, or even muffins lingering in the air."

"I've been waiting for an invite. Will it be a public space or baking central?"

"Just my bakery, but I'll be open for special visitors from time to time who might need a sample." I pushed back my chair. "Come on. It's not much to look at now but maybe you'll get the idea." Josie stood and Hank sat up in his bed, tail wagging.

"You stay here, little man. There might be a rogue nail or two on the floor." He laid his head down on his paws and looked up through his little eyelashes as if he knew exactly what I had said, or maybe it was the word stay. We'd been working on that one for a year now with a modicum of success.

I pulled open the connecting door to the former housekeeper's apartment. "It's not large, but it'll be suitable for what I have in mind. At least until the brick and mortar bakery is rebuilt."

We entered what had been the living room and kitchen. Bare studs wrapped the space and the wood floor was stripped of carpet and linoleum, exposing exquisite mahogany hardwood. "We have to rewire to replace this tube and rod electrical, insulate, and then we can sheetrock the walls, seal the floor, and get appliances."

Casey chuckled. "That's all? Let me guess, you'll be baking by next weekend?"

"Not quite. Structurally the space is sound, so that helps speed up the timeline."

Josie cocked her head. "What's that paper on the floor near the back door?"

"Russ must have forgotten it." I crossed the room and picked it up. As I scanned the page, my gut tightened.

"What is it, Temperance?" Casey asked.

"Last night was planned." I reviewed it one more time as if it would change the typed words on the page.

"Get girls to make up. Get a small container. Find an excuse to drop by. Hang around until the deed is done. Take care of G." I looked up. "This is a checklist for murder."

12

———————

I handed Casey the paper. "What do you make of it?"

She didn't speak for several moments. Then, holding it up for Josie to read she said, "It's exactly what you said. Someone made a plan and executed it. The deed was killing Franny. But here's a question that's been rolling around in my brain. Why not kill Gloria too? She was there, and we can surmise she was attacked at the house since that's where we found her car. Once she was unconscious, it would have been easy to finish her off." She grimaced, "Not to sound crass."

"Couldn't the deed refer to both ladies, and G could be Gordon?" Josie said, "Whoever did this hoped Gloria would drown. As Temperance said earlier, it appeared that she had gone night fishing. It would have been easy to have a misstep and fall in, get pulled by the current, hit her head and be swept over the waterfalls." Her cheeks flushed. "Well she didn't say all of that, I added in a few thoughts of my own."

I smiled. "That's what this investigation is about, facts and theories. Well done, Josie."

"Thanks."

Glancing at Casey I asked, "Is there anyone we can cross off our list of suspects at this point?"

She said, "I don't see how. We need to question everyone at the station and track down alibis. That includes Chase, Seth, Kelly and Gordon. We know he saw Franny at some point between the time he delivered the pizza and before she died. He needs to confirm the time and if anyone was loitering near her house."

"Unless Gordon is the killer."

Josie's lips thinned. "If he were, he'd also be responsible for attacking Gloria. They're close. I can't see him hurting her."

Casey said, "I've seen worse things from families."

Nodding, I sighed. "So have I. But I'm going to hold onto good thoughts that Gordon saw something and can help us."

"Where do we go from here?" Josie asked.

I placed a hand on my chest. "I'm waiting until shift change at the Quickie Mart to see if I can get any information from the clerk."

"Why's that?"

Josie said, "Temperance thinks someone could have talked to Gloria when she stopped for ice cream and night crawlers."

"And can you pull the security footage for last night? If someone did approach her or follow her, it'd be caught on camera."

"There's a little problem with that idea." Casey shifted from one foot to the other. "The system saves the footage on a rolling basis, for twelve hours. It was taped over by nine this morning. Maybe you should let the officers handle questioning the clerk when he comes on duty."

I groaned. "You have got to be kidding me. Doesn't the owner realize that it's better to have files saved for thirty days in case of shoplifters or other problems?"

"He doesn't want to pay for that. He's a cheap dude from what his employees have said."

I perked up. "Did you talk to who was working last night?"

She shook her head. "No. There have been other incidents at the Mart. As you mentioned, shoplifting and people skipping out on paying for gas are why you now have to pay first before pumping. No more honor system. Then of course there's the occasional altercation between patrons or the underage kid trying to buy a six-pack of beer."

"What kind of convenience store is he running?" Josie asked.

"One that skirts the gray areas of the law."

Her eyes bugged out. "Casey, are you saying he's knowingly selling alcohol to minors?"

"Not him directly, but we suspect someone is, we just can't catch them. Yet. But we will. You can count on that. Which is why any information we glean from them should be treated with a dash of skepticism."

Josie folded her arms over her chest. "Suddenly, I'm realizing that under the surface Oak Hollow has a less-than-sparkly reputation. I'm so naïve."

I placed my hand on her shoulder. "You're not. Trusting is one word that comes to mind, and you think the best of everybody. That's something I admire about you, Josie. Since we met as kids, I've known you have a huge heart. You accepted me."

"Well, thanks, but right now I think it's me being foolish."

Casey said, "I believe in people until proven wrong, and I think that's why I like you and Temperance. You believe the best in people until you have concrete evidence to the contrary."

I smiled. "Thanks, that's nice to hear." My arm swept the space. "Anyway, to wrap up the tour of two-point-o, on the back wall ovens will be installed with a stainless-steel work station in the center. The other walls will be lined with shelves for supplies and the wall which abuts the bathroom will be the sink and dishwasher. I kept the bedroom as my office. It doesn't need much work, a fresh coat of paint and they've ripped up the carpet and it will get the same treatment as the rest of the space."

"Are you redoing the bathroom?" Casey peeked her head in there.

"Not now. There's no reason to. It's functional."

Nodding, she said, "This space has a good vibe."

"I can't take all the credit. Josie spurred me along."

She rubbed her hands together. "My only request: I want the first loaf of bread that comes out of this kitchen."

I laughed. "You got it." I pointed to the door. "We should go back to the kitchen. There's not much more to see here."

"Any chance I could have a Ziploc baggie? I'd like to take this note into custody since it seems tied to my case."

"Help yourself. They're in the pantry cabinet, right-hand side, third shelf."

I cleared the table of our dinner dishes as I thought about the note. Who had been in the apartment last? It was a question for Russ. My heart stilled. Could he have something to do with all of this? He had been in and out of the apartment over the last several days. He could have overheard the argument and he was only a few years older than Josie and the others. "Josie, did Russ Patterson go to school with you?"

She plunked down in a chair and shook her head. "Don't go there. Not everyone who was here yesterday is a suspect."

Casey looked up. "Well, yeah they are. Why are you asking about Russ?"

"I'm wondering how well he knew everyone and what his relationship was to the garden center and the farm?"

Josie again shook her head. "He's older than us and served in the Army for eight to ten years before moving back. He wasn't around when the fires happened. Therefore, he has no motive. Besides, the man is nuts about you. Even if he had done something wrong, there's no way he would have dropped a clue at your place. He'd never implicate you as a litterbug with a gum wrapper on the ground."

"Temperance, it's fantastic that you're keeping an open mind but in Russ's case, there isn't anything tying him to the crimes. Josie's right; that man's interested in you."

I wasn't ready to admit that he caused my heart to skip a beat or three. "Alright, I'm just talking out loud to keep all the facts relevant." Lifting the lid from the cake stand I said, "Let's have dessert and put talk of murder and assault on the back burner."

Josie grinned and Casey asked, "Do you have any ice cream?"

Sitting on the porch as the sun began her descent to the horizon, we chatted about the bakery menu after enjoying dessert.

Casey said, "I'm sure the Early Rise 2.0 will be a smash success."

"I'm looking forward to not working as hard as I did with the brick and mortar store. Russ, the electrician, and the plumber will be over tomorrow. They'll get it all roughed in this week, I hope."

Casey stretched her arms overhead. "I'm going to take off and get a quick nap before I go on duty at midnight." She stood. "Are you still going to go to the convenience store and poke around?" Her gaze zipped from Josie to me.

First, I went for the innocent routine and shrugged. "I'm out of ice cream."

She tipped her head and studied me.

"Do you object?"

Casey's brows knitted together, and her eye contact with me was intense. "Would it do any good if I did?"

Josie laughed. "Probably not, but I'll go with Temperance as backup or at least a second pair of eyes."

"Then stay alert, be careful, and of course if you uncover

anything important, call me right away. If you get in a bind, call 9-1-1. This killer wants to cover his tracks."

"If that's true, then why leave the car at Franny's? Wouldn't he have taken it back to Gloria's place?" Josie said.

I said, "Josie has a good point. Why did he leave the car there?"

"He could have had a twinge of guilt and hoped Gloria would be found and be attended to."

"Casey, is that your way of saying find her body for closure?"

She lifted her shoulder. "Possible. At this point, all we have are questions with zero answers. Hopefully tomorrow we'll get something more from the coroner about the exact cause of death. We're bringing everyone in for questioning in the morning."

I opened my mouth.

Holding up her hand, she said, "Before you ask no, you may not be there during our interviews. They've been scheduled to start at eight o'clock. If you'd like to have lunch, I'll share with you what I can."

I did some quick thinking. "While you're doing the interviews I can take a run out to the garden center and maybe even the landscape office."

"You're not leaving me out of the fun. I'm coming with you," Josie said.

I gave her a wink. "That goes without saying. We'll be on alert and call if we discover anything important before lunch."

Casey asked, "I can't order you to stand down, but I'd like to. Besides, I've seen what you can do with a little persistence in your way of asking questions. Just be careful. And yes, I've said that twice in the last few minutes but I mean it."

"Before you go, were there prints on the EpiPen that was discovered outside?"

"Just Franny's."

"The killer wore gloves." I pressed my fingers to my eyes, frustrated each time I thought we might catch a break.

"I hate to ask an ignorant question but would the kind of gloves matter?" Josie looked at Casey.

"Fabric or latex would obscure fingerprints. Why do you ask?"

I nodded. "Landscapers wear gloves, that would include Kelly and Chase."

Josie said, "And mechanics sometimes do too."

She was right. Did that narrow the pool or suspects? "The only people who don't wear gloves on a regular basis are Gordon and Seth."

"Well, Seth plays golf and he uses a glove for that."

Casey asked, "Josie, are you sure about Seth?"

"Yes, he was on the golf league in school, and he was good."

"Only Gordon doesn't wear them regularly. Can you get a search warrant for their vehicles?"

She shook her head. "I'd need more concrete evidence. Warrants aren't for fishing expeditions." She looked at her watch. "I gotta take off." She walked down the front steps. "Call if you need me."

I stood and crossed to the railing. "Will do." Hank whined at the screen door. Josie let him out onto the porch.

Casey backed out of the drive. I glanced over my shoulder. "I thought we'd drive over to the Quickie Mart in about a half hour. Care to go for a short walk with me and Hank?"

"Sure. Maybe we can swing by my house so I can turn on a few outside lights. That way when I get home it won't be completely dark." She shivered. "All this talk of someone we know committing these crimes is unnerving."

I slipped my arm around her shoulder and gave her a one-armed hug. "You don't need to go with me."

She gave me a side eye. "Are you kidding? And miss you poking around, asking discreet questions and honing in on a speck of information that could turn this case upside down? Not a chance."

Hank danced at our feet and I scooped him up and kissed his velvety soft ears. "Did you hear that, Hank? Josie's ready for another adventure. But first, it's a sniff fest for you."

He gave a sharp bark and his tail thumped my side.

I set him down and opened the screen to the house. " Let's get your harness and we'll go."

Josie waited on the front porch. When I carried Hank down the steps and set him on the front walk, we strolled through the picket fence gate.

"When are you going to repaint the old flower cart you want to use for your bakery stand?"

"This week, I'm going to sand it down. Russ offered to put a roof on it and a few shelves. Then I need replacement wheels, the old metal is out of round, and it's difficult to move it."

"Do you need to move it? Why can't you put some land-scape fabric down with some plants and leave it in one spot?"

I grinned. "Josie, that's a great idea. Let's hit up the garden center tomorrow, and maybe we can bump into Kelly. She could make some recommendations and put me on their schedule to redo the front lawn."

Her brow wrinkled. "You don't have to go to all that trouble. It's something we could do, it's a small area."

"Oh, no we couldn't. It's a business expense, and I want it to be professional." I gave her a sly wink, just in case anyone was lurking behind any bushes as we passed the shortcut to South Street from Mahogany. It was just a few days ago that I discovered it was a good place to get lost if necessary, which my friend Jonah had been using to come to my place, and he was stabbed.

A gleam came into her eye when she got my double meaning. "Oh. Right. We should talk to the professionals. You'll need something that's low maintenance while looking amazing with the bakery cart as the focal point."

I nodded and dropped my voice. "Of course while we're there a few well-placed casual questions would be appropriate."

Josie grabbed my arm and nodded up the street. Gordon was getting a pizza out of his hatchback. "Are you thinking what I'm thinking?"

He hurried up the walk and knocked on the Walker's front door. "Pizza delivery."

I urged Hank forward and by the time Gordon had concluded his business with Mrs. Walker we were waiting by his car.

"Hello Gordon," I said.

"Hey Temperance, Josie. I don't have a delivery for you tonight." His eyes darted to his car.

"No, we didn't order. I wanted to thank you again for taking the last of the cupcakes off my hands yesterday. Who did you end up giving them to?"

"One box went to Henrietta, she was still at the restaurant when I got back, one to the waitress at Sassy's, and later I gave a box to Franny and Gloria."

"What time did you stop by Franny's place?"

"Around seven, I think." He pointed to his car. "I gotta run, hot pizzas in the back, and if they're cold when I deliver them, there's trouble from the boss."

I stepped to the side, allowing him to get in his car. "Drive carefully, and thanks again for distributing the cupcakes. I hope Henrietta gives me a great write-up."

"Don't worry about that Temperance, she will. They're the best."

13

I pulled my SUV up to the gas pump in front of the Quickie Mart. I looked at the front door. "Okay, we want to know if the clerk remembers seeing Gloria last night and what she bought. It's a long shot but worth the ask."

Josie nodded. "Are you getting gas?"

"Yes, I want to walk through this like any other customer might have, namely Gloria."

"Got it." Josie pushed open her door. "Should I wait for you before going in?"

"No. Go ahead and wander around, maybe chat up the clerk for a minute. Ask if he was busy last night, that kind of thing."

"You got it."

"I'll be in as soon as I'm done." We both got out, I opened the gas cap and set the nozzle in while scanning the area, looking at what the cameras could see. They had a good view of the pumps and the parking area for the store. The pump stopped, and I took my receipt. Now, inside surveillance. My heart rate kicked up. Maybe I should have been a field agent instead of a data analyst. This part was intriguing. Another memory flashed, and my gut flipped. I pushed it aside, there was no time to think about that last case. Not today, or maybe ever.

The door chimed when I opened it. That was good, there was no way to sneak in. I nodded to the older man behind the counter. I could see over the racks of snack foods, magazines, vehicle basics, and the coffee and soda machines to the row of refrigerated items against the back and side walls.

Josie looked up and waved to me. "Ice cream?"

I strolled over, feeling the clerk's eyes on my back. "Anything interesting catch your eye?"

"Yes. Come see for yourself." She had the door closed, and I pretended to study the shelf. Keeping my voice soft, I said, "Anything?"

"He's been watching me like a hawk. If this is his norm, he would have noticed all the details about Gloria last night."

"Let's choose a couple of pints and check out." I glanced up. Like Russ said, there were big screens in each corner of the shop.

I grabbed a pint of Double Mint Chip and selected a chocolate-covered strawberry for Josie. I had to taste that one, since chocolate and strawberries were a weakness of mine.

We approached the counter. The man's name tag read Keith.

I gave him a wide smile as I set my pint on the counter. "Hi Keith, how are you doing tonight?"

He nodded. "Fine thanks. Will this be all?"

Josie set her pint down too.

"Yes, thanks, but I was wondering if you could tell me what kind of ice cream my friend bought last night. She was in around eight. You might remember her, she also bought some worms."

He looked at the ceiling and then said, "I know who you're talking about. Her name's Gloria and she usually buys her bait here. Last night she bought two containers and two pints, one Vanilla Bean and the other Rocky Road. But isn't she the gal who was found down by the river, she'd gotten conked on the head?"

Which way should I play this, like I didn't know, or that I was concerned? "That's her. I wanted to pick up her favorite ice cream and drop it off."

"That's nice of you. She's a nice girl who stops in at least once a week for bait and she likes Rocky Road the best."

Josie pointed to the freezer case. "I'll grab one."

"Thanks. If you could add that, I'd appreciate it."

He tapped a few keys and said the total. I handed him a twenty. "Was there anyone else in the store at the same time? Maybe someone who was bothering her?"

He glanced up without moving his head as he counted out my change. "Are you a cop?"

"No, sir. Just a concerned friend."

"You're that baker lady, the one whose business just burned down. There's an article on you in this morning's edition of the Oak Hollow Gazette. Henrietta Wells wrote a nice piece on you."

"Really?" I looked at the stack of newspapers. "I'll take one of those too."

He kept a dollar of the change in his hand. "She does a nice job with the stuff she writes."

Josie came back. "Found the Rocky Road."

"Thanks for the tip. I had heard she might write something, but I had no idea it'd be that fast."

"Most likely she was looking for a good story, and that was a doozie. I wish you good luck with two-point-o."

"So Keith, was anyone in here at the same time that Gloria was, maybe he followed her to the car?"

"Nope. It was quiet like a church in here last night. Gloria stopped around eight and like I said, she bought ice cream and bait, and then around ten a couple of people bought gas but they used credit cards, so they didn't come into the store. It was uneventful. I closed at eleven on the dot."

"Thank you, Keith."

"You're welcome and tell Gloria I hope she feels better soon."

I gave him a quizzical look.

He pressed his lips flat. "When you drop off the ice cream."

"Right, we're going there right now and we'll be sure to tell her you were asking about her."

"Good." He watched us as we got into my SUV and buckled up.

"We're going to swing by Gloria's and drop off the ice cream just in case he checks up on us since he seems to know her pretty well."

Josie slid her window down and waved to him. "Good idea."

We eased from the gas pumps and I turned right out of the parking lot. "Should we call first or just drop by?"

Her brow arched. "It might be interesting to cruise up and see if anything is going on that might be useful. And then I was thinking, what if we drove through Franny's neighborhood too?"

I grinned. "I was already planning that drive-by. Hattie and Babette might be doing their neighborhood watch thing and we could offer them some pints of ice cream too."

"That's if we don't stay long at Gloria's, otherwise they'll be liquid before we get back to Franny's."

"Behind my seat is a small cooler. Pop them in there. That'll help."

"Were you a scout as a kid?"

"No, but I like to be prepared. Call it an annoying trait leftover from the past." I clenched the wheel and sped up.

Josie fell silent, and for that I was grateful. I needed to mull over what we had learned, and figure out if there was any subtext I might've overlooked. We arrived at Gloria's in no time.

The street was quiet as Josie tapped on the front door. In the falling darkness, the light from the living room windows illuminated the steps. We should have called but I was looking for the element of surprise.

Chase pulled the door open. "Ladies, this is unexpected."

I couldn't read the expression on his face. "Hi Chase, sorry to bother you but we were out for a drive and thought you and Gloria might like some ice cream." I held up the cooler. "We'll only stay for a minute or two."

He called over his shoulder. "Glo, it's Josie and Temperance. They brought us ice cream. Is it okay if they come in?"

I strained to hear her response. "Of course."

He pushed open the screen. "You might be just the distraction she needs. It's almost eight and that's when she left to drive over to my sister's." Tears pooled in his eyes and he blinked them away. Stepping back from the doorway, he ushered us in.

Gloria was in the same chair as when we had left. "How are you feeling?" Josie bent over and gave her a half hug.

"It's good to be home but I'm still numb. Franny. Dead." She shook her head. "I can't comprehend why anyone would want to hurt her. She's sweet-tempered. I'm the hot head of the duo."

Chase took her hand. His voice softened, "Even yours is tame compared to most people. Take me for example. I get upset and explode."

I perked up. Chase had a temper? Interesting.

"Chase, I meant to thank you for all you did to help me yesterday."

"It was a few hours, Temperance, no big deal. It was great to see so many people stop and help. Russ does a good job rustling up volunteers for events like this."

I made a mental note that I could repay all the kindness showered on me over the last week or so if Russ does this kind of thing often. "I'll bet you were tired last night."

"Not really. Seth and I went out to the drag way for a few hours. We thought we'd bump into Jacob. There's nothing like fast cars, loud engines, and hanging with friends to wrap up a busy day."

"I've never been. Do the races end early?"

He chuckled. "Nope. Last night I think we got home just after midnight. There were a few special races we didn't want to miss. One was this jet truck that ran the quarter mile. It takes like three minutes to gear up to run it, and then at over one hundred eighty miles an hour. BAM!" He clapped his hands together. "That was all he wrote."

Gloria gave him a tender smile. "He loves everything to do with fast cars."

He covered his face with his hands as if he had just made the correlation. "If I hadn't gone, Franny might still be alive and you wouldn't have gotten hurt."

"Chase, if you hadn't gone to the drag race, you wouldn't have been eating cupcakes and drinking wine with us."

I gave Josie a side glance. There weren't any wine glasses sitting on the tables, but there were three in the dish drainer.

Josie said, "Chase, she's right. You would have been doing your own thing. What happened last night isn't your fault."

Silence fell over the room as he rushed out. I heard the back door slam.

Tears slid down Gloria's face. "He's been like this off and on all day today. I get it, but it doesn't have anything to do with him."

"What does it have to do with, Gloria? What's the secret you and Franny were arguing about in my front yard?"

The tears continued to stream over her cheeks. Josie handed her a tissue from the box on the side table.

"I made a promise that I'd never tell anyone. We were taking it to our graves and now Franny has."

"Someone else knows, though. It wasn't just about you and Franny anymore. Whoever did this discovered the secret and, for some reason, wanted to silence you both. Why?" I didn't intend to be stern with her but it was imperative to crack the turtle shell that she had pulled around this secret.

In a hushed whisper she said, "By accident, we discovered who started the greenhouse and barn fires."

"Why didn't you take that information to the authorities?" Josie asked.

"We were scared."

"How did you find out?" My tone was more gentle now that I had gotten this far. The rest should come out in a soft whoosh of details.

"Years ago, when I first fell in love with fishing we were at the wormhole, and there was this rocky outcropping under the tree canopy. It's far enough away from the bank that I don't think the spring thaw reached it. I guess if there was ever a real flood it might."

I gave her the time she needed to tell her story even though I wanted to pummel her with questions and then call Casey.

"Sorry, I love that place. The fish weren't biting so why not explore? Franny and I were poking around and we came across a journal in a waterproof bag. You know the kind that people use when they go camping or hiking?"

I nodded. "Go on."

"The first time we found it we didn't read it. I thought someone just forgot it and would come back. You know I didn't want to read anyone's private thoughts. But we kept checking all summer and on a dare, we read it."

Josie asked, "Was there a name inside the journal?"

"No. We didn't figure out who's it was, at least not right away. We read the entries over the next few weeks. At first it was boring stuff - talking about bike rides, summer jobs, going back to school, that kind of thing. But then we read about the barn fire and we got scared. This person was mad and burned it down out of spite. They weren't making enough in their summer job on the farm."

"Had you figured out by that time who it was?"

She shook her head and grimaced. "Not then. The barn fire was the last entry. We put it back and never mentioned it again until the following summer. When we went back to the same place, we looked to see if the journal was there."

"And it was?" I asked.

She nodded. "This time it talked about the greenhouse fire. There was one sentence that made it obvious who it was."

Chase rushed into the house. "We need to get out of here. The beehive—they're mad as all get out. They're all over the place out there."

"And Chase is allergic!" Gloria struggled to get to her feet. He pulled her into his arms. I raced to the front door with Josie right behind me. "I'll back my vehicle up so you can get in."

I raced to the SUV. I could hear the hum of the hive. This wasn't good at all. How the heck did that happen? Was Chase the one who aggravated the nest?

Tires squealed and taillights glowed on the bend up ahead as I drew open the driver's door, Josie hopped into the passenger seat, and I threw it in reverse. I didn't care about the damage to the lawn. My focus was to get Gloria and Chase out of that house as fast as possible.

Josie jumped out when I came to a rolling stop, pulled open the back door while Chase pushed Gloria inside, and he jumped in after her.

"Go!" he cried.

I floored it and didn't dare look at Josie, but said, "Call Casey and have her meet us at the police station."

14

———————

I checked my rearview mirror and was grateful that we left the angry hive behind. "Tell Casey to put out a neighborhood alert to be wary of aggressive bees."

With another look in the rearview, I saw that Chase had his arm around Gloria whose head was buried in his shoulder. I nodded out the windshield. "Keep your eyes peeled."

Josie held up her finger and pointed to her ear and cell. "Casey? Josie. Any chance you can meet us at the police station? We have Chase and Gloria with us. There was an incident at her place. Also, if there is such a thing, put out an alert about a bee hive being agitated."

With a glance in my direction, she nodded. "Yes. We'll be there in ten minutes." Another longer pause, before saying, "Right. Bye."

"Casey will be at the station. She said if we get there before she does go inside and wait in the lobby."

I wanted to ask what else she had said but if Josie wasn't volunteering the information, it must not be for everyone's ears. Patience was the habit I needed to practice now.

"How are you both doing back there?"

Chase's eyes met mine in the mirror. "Okay. Thanks for helping us."

"Do you have any idea what happened?" I asked.

He shook his head. "Bees don't get aggressive at night unless they believe their home is under attack. They felt threatened."

Josie asked, "Do you know a lot about bee behavior?"

"After I discovered my allergy was life threatening, I studied up on them to make sure I knew how to avoid dying." He glanced out the window. "Sorry if that sounds harsh given the circumstances, but Franny knew about bees too. She had never been stung until April, when she was walking in the grass and stepped on one. Before she went to the emergency room, she took some over the counter antihistamine which gave her some time to drive herself since she was home alone. Once she knew, she had EpiPens everywhere - in her purse, car, work, the kitchen, bathroom, heck even her bedroom. That girl was over-prepared."

That didn't track with what was found when her house was searched. "Is that when the beehive at Gloria's was discovered, in April?"

"Yeah. Despite our issues, we understand the importance of bee health in our world. Gloria decided to wait until they swarmed this fall and then have the tree removed so a new queen wouldn't move in."

"Weren't you scared living so close to a hive that large?" Josie asked.

Gloria said, "If you respect them, they won't attack you just because you exist. It's not like a carnivore hunting for food. In fact, the ironic thing is that I had planted more pollinators in the gardens to feed them and hired someone to mow the lawn. Franny had done the same thing."

"Chase, you didn't do it for her?"

He shook his head. "She didn't want to put me at risk. If a stray stone ejected from the mower and hit the hive, that would have riled them up. She said the family discount wasn't worth the risk."

"Franny sounds like an amazing sister."

"The best."

Gloria sniffled. "She had a heart of gold."

Josie and I continued to scan the road in front and on the sides, and I kept an eye on the rearview mirror. What had that vehicle been doing so close to Gloria's and with their headlights off? But Chase knew a lot about bees. Would he have taken the chance to tick off the hive to stop Gloria from talking? One bee sting, an EpiPen could handle, but multiple stings, probably not. That could be lethal. My hands tightened on the wheel as I shook my head.

Josie's forehead wrinkled, her eyes drawn together and her mouth pursed. She was as perplexed as I was.

We drove the rest of the way in silence. Gloria's tears had subsided. Chase held her in his arms, and Josie stared out the windows, head swiveling like an owl.

I parked in the closest space to the well-lit main entrance at the police station. "Everyone ready?" The car pulling away from the house was sketchy but now nowhere to be seen.

Chase said, "Ready." I got out and opened the back door. Gloria slid out first and then Chase. Josie jogged around the back of the SUV and ran up the steps to open the door.

Clutching Chase's hand Gloria said with a catch in her voice, "I'm so sorry all this has happened."

"Hush. You didn't do anything wrong other than let Franny convince you to keep that journal a secret, but she was trying to do what she thought was right." He kissed her forehead. "Don't worry. We'll get through this together."

My heart constricted. It was apparent how much this man loved Gloria, but could he be responsible for what had happened? Not that he'd kill his sister, but might he have played an unwitting role in this debacle? I didn't know.

Chase wrapped his arm around Gloria's waist as they

climbed the cement steps. I followed behind them, staying alert, but everything was quiet. Josie walked in behind me. I crossed to the desk. "We're supposed to meet Officer Butler."

He nodded. "She called ahead and asked that I put you in an interview room."

It was the best place. No exterior windows for anyone to see who was where. Even if we hadn't been followed here, the arsonist/murderer would guess this is where we'd come.

We followed the desk officer down a corridor. The linoleum floor was beige like the painted cement walls. He stepped through a metal door that had half wire glass into a room that contained a metal rectangular table and six matching chairs. There was not one forgiving surface in sight.

"Can I get anyone a bottle of water?"

I nodded. "That would be nice, thank you."

He closed the door with a thud. Gloria flashed Chase a panicked look as she continued to cling to his hand with a claw-like grip. "I'm frightened."

"We're safe here." His attempt to reassure seemed to help as she exhaled a ragged breath.

"We should sit," Josie said. "Casey will be here soon."

"Why did you bring us here?" Chase asked.

I nodded to Gloria. "She has a few things to share with Casey. Besides, I don't think the bees getting all stirred up after dark was a coincidence. Someone may have been outside the house listening to our conversation."

Gloria's hand flew to her mouth. "So they might know that I know who did..." she threw up her hands, "everything?"

"It's possible. I think it's best to be here for the time being."

He turned his chair to face Gloria. "Do you know who killed Franny?"

She dropped her head. "I know who burned the green-house and my grandparents' barn. Years ago, we found a journal. The writer never said specifically who they were, but we figured it out."

He turned his head, got up, and paced the length of the small room and back. "Why would you keep it a secret? Property was destroyed."

"We were terrified that if we told anyone what we discovered, something bad would happen."

"Like this?"

She recoiled at the bite in his words. "Chase, Franny was insistent we stay quiet. You know how she was."

"Then why were you talking about it yesterday? Is that what you were arguing about?"

She nodded, her eyes glued to the beige floor. "Yes. When we learned about the fire at the bakery and that it was arson we wondered if it was the same person. After the arrest was made, Franny couldn't shake the dread she carried. Now she wanted to tell the truth, and I was scared. Words were exchanged and honestly, we never thought anyone was paying attention to us."

"The arsonist was." He dropped into his chair. "I don't blame you for what happened. You're a victim in this, too. I lost my sister, but I could have lost you too. I wouldn't have been able to draw another breath until I knew why."

Josie said, "Chase, Franny and Gloria were just kids when this happened. Put yourself in their shoes."

He said, "I'm trying. It's hard when I'm sitting here looking at Glo, with her head sporting a bunch of stitches and covered with insect bites from spending the night at the water's edge. How am I supposed to be all easy breezy, not to mention my sister is dead and I have to arrange a funeral tomorrow?"

"What about your parents?" I asked gently.

"Mom left when we were kids and Dad has early-onset dementia and lives in a long-term care facility. I told him about Franny, but he didn't understand what happened. He doesn't even recognize me. Taking care of Franny is my responsibility."

"You're not alone, Chase." Gloria held his hand.

It was sweet how they continued to support each other. Extreme circumstances like these either pull a couple apart or push them closer together. I hoped it would be the latter for these two. It was easy to see how deeply they cared for each other. "If you need anything, I'd be happy to help."

Josie said, "Me too. You don't have to shoulder this burden alone."

He nodded his thanks as he wiped his cheeks with the back of his hand.

"Chase, who was Franny dating? I understand she and Seth broke up a while back."

With a lift of his shoulder he said, "No idea. Do you know, Gloria?"

"The only thing she told me was that this someone might be her forever guy. She said it was so new that she didn't want to rush it by telling me too quickly."

I glanced at Josie. "Normally, would she hold back news like that?"

She shook her head. "No, but what does that have to do with last night?"

"Maybe nothing," I said. Or maybe a great deal.

A sharp rap on the door preceded Casey striding into the room. She looked at each person and ended with me. "Sorry to make you wait. It took longer than I thought to get back."

"That's not a problem. Chase and Gloria have been talking about things."

She cocked a brow, pulled out a chair, and sat. No one spoke. She cleared her throat. "What happened tonight?"

I gave Gloria a pointed look.

She shook her head. "Temperance, you tell her."

I took a deep breath, giving her another opportunity to speak. When she didn't I said, "Josie and I went out for ice cream, and we decided to take Gloria and Chase a couple of pints. While we were talking, Chase went outside for some air."

He turned his head to stare at the wall.

Casey asked, "You were talking about Franny?"

Gloria looked at the floor. "Yes. About everything."

"We were discussing the secret the girls have been keeping for years, and the importance for Gloria to give you the details. Chase rushed into the house and said he thought the bees were going to swarm."

"The bees in the hollow tree behind Gloria's?"

"The same." Chase said, "They would only get angry at night if they felt they needed to protect the hive. It was too dark and I couldn't see, but I felt we had to leave the house."

Casey nodded. "You're deathly allergic."

"One sting and the EpiPen will give me time to get to the hospital, but who knows the outcome if I was stung multiple times?"

"What happened next?"

Josie said, "Temperance backed her SUV up to the door so that Chase and Gloria could get in, just in case. We didn't want a scene out of a horror movie."

"I couldn't take the chance of Chase getting stung. But when I got in my car, I heard tires screeching and saw tail-lights sans headlights racing away from the curb."

Casey's eyes flicked wide and if I hadn't been watching her closely, I would have missed her tell of surprise as she maintained her stoic stance. "Were you able to get the make or model of the vehicle?"

"No. It was too dark."

"We watched for anyone following us on the way here. But we didn't see a car or truck," Josie said.

"Temperance, you think whoever was in that car knew about the bees and did something to rile them up?"

Nodding, I said, "It fits. Sneaking around, doing just

enough to make things happen. Like staging Gloria's fishing equipment at the river.

She scoffed. "Yeah, about that. You said there was a bait container with my equipment and my headlamp for night fishing. Whoever did that doesn't know a thing about it. Night crawlers?"

"That's a good point," Chase said, "He or she wouldn't be a fishing person."

Josie said, "I like to drop a line, but had no idea worms wouldn't work at night."

"How many of your friends go night fishing?" I asked. Since my list of suspects was connected to Franny and Gloria, they willingly had protected this person for years, he or she had to be a friend, even if they weren't close.

"Chase and I are the only ones who do."

He nodded. "It's really peaceful, and we love the sounds of nature at night. The outdoors wakes up. It's magical."

Casey leaned closer to Gloria. "Tell me how you thought you knew who the arsonist was."

Gloria said, "Franny and I found a journal near the riverbank after my grandparents lost their barn. Over time we read it, and then the following year after the greenhouse fire, we found it again and saw that the person wrote about watching the fire burn. They wrote about the raw power of flames consuming the wood. That is a direct quote and one I never could forget. Like, who writes about *raw power*? Before you ask why we didn't turn the journal over to the cops, remember we were a couple of scared teenagers, and we didn't want to be involved. What if the person found out it was us who turned them in? We didn't want to get hurt or worse."

Casey's face was a mask. "What happened to the journal?"

She shrugged. "We put it back where we found it; at the wormhole fishing spot."

"When was that?"

"The summer we graduated from high school."

"That was ten years ago," Josie whispered.

"Would you show us in the morning?" Casey asked. "It's a long shot but worth exploring."

"Sure. Will Chase be able to come with me?" She hadn't let go of his hand since they sat down at the table.

"Yes. But he'll have to stand clear when told."

He said, "That I can do."

"Now, Gloria." Casey's face was stern. "Who wrote in the journal?"

Nervously, she licked her lips and stared at Casey. "Do you think that person killed Franny and attacked me?"

"It's a strong possibility, which is why you need to tell me everything you know."

She wrenched her hand from Chase and covered her face as sobs wracked her body. "I, I Can't."

15

Casey nodded to the door and Josie and I followed her into the hall. Once the door was closed she turned to us.

"I can't protect her if she doesn't trust me."

The frustration in Casey's voice echoed how I felt. "Agreed. Gloria did the same thing when she was talking to us. She gets right to the point of saying who she thinks wrote the journal and then clams up."

Josie asked, "What if the reason she does that is because it's Gordon? They're related, and maybe that's why she hesitates. It's one thing to know the person who committed these horrible crimes, but another if it's a member of your family."

Casey asked, "Temperance, what's your gut telling you?"

"Based on the little information we have? Josie could be correct. I know if it were me, I'd be reluctant to name a relative. However, I also wouldn't withhold that information either."

"How do we get her to spill the beans?" Josie asked.

"I'm going to question her about last night. This morning at the hospital I asked questions with little results, but tonight changes everything. I have to put pressure on her. Temperance, how do you feel about being the good person in the room? I'll be tough, and maybe even Josie could chime in and strongly suggest Gloria tell us everything? I want to protect her and Chase, but they're tying my hands."

Josie and I nodded. "We'll help," I said. "The desk officer was going to get bottled water, but he must have gotten tied up. Do you think we can take in a few bottles? This conversation might take a bit."

"Go back inside and I'll bring some in."

When we walked in, Chase held Gloria in his arms. He looked up, tears wetting his cheeks. "We were talking about the funeral."

"Casey is getting bottled water."

Josie said, "Have you come to any decisions? About the funeral?"

"Not really, just that we want lots of flowers and everyone has to dress in bright colors and vibrant patterns."

Gloria gave us a weak smile. "Franny wouldn't want us to dress in all black. She hated it when we paid our respects at funerals, and everyone looked like they were going to a funeral. Which they were but she always said a life should be celebrated, not mourned."

He nodded. "I'll miss her every day, but I'll do my best to honor her for the rest of my life."

"That's a wonderful outlook." I wondered if maybe the reality of his sister's death hadn't fully impacted him yet. In time, it would hit him hard.

Gloria said, "Me too."

As if I cued her, Casey entered the room and placed bottles of water on the table before she took a seat.

"Gloria, we need to talk about last night. I get the feeling you're holding something back."

She unscrewed a cap from a bottle and sipped.

Gloria said, "I've told you everything I remember."

Under Casey's unflinching gaze, Gloria squirmed in the

chair. Casey said, "Tell me about the argument with Franny. What set you off at Temperance's house?"

Gloria said, "Franny's always been afraid of fire. When we started talking about the bakery, which was natural considering we were helping get the new space ready, she got that look in her eye she would get whenever she thought about what we knew."

"What look?"

So far, this conversation had been between Casey and Gloria. Josie and I remained silent, and Chase watched Gloria.

"Her nostrils would flare, and she didn't blink. Almost as if her eyes were frozen open, and then she'd start to hum offbeat."

"And you knew she was thinking about the journal, remembering the barn or greenhouse?"

"All of it. Her fear of him finding out started about three months after we read the last journal entry. We were going to college in a couple of weeks and she thought that if we weren't together, something bad would happen. I was going to be going to school in Boston, and she was going to Rhode Island."

What happened?"

"I transferred mid-year and got an apartment off campus. Franny moved in and we spent the next four years living together. It got easier for her, and she almost forgot about it until the bakery fire last week."

Chase said, "I never understood why you transferred schools. You were a good friend to Franny."

Gloria looked at him. "My best friend needed me and since we made the decision together to keep the secret, I had to support her."

That was a profound connection. I said, "My fire brought it all back?"

"Yes. After the arrest was made we talked about the past. I thought we should come forward. Obviously, no one had been arrested for the crimes. Franny's fear got the best of her yesterday morning and it bubbled over. We weren't paying attention to who was around when she blurted out, '*I don't care what you say. We're never exposing the truth about those fires. I'll take that secret to my grave.*'"

"Do you know who was closest to you during the argument?" Casey asked.

She bit the inside of her cheek. "I wasn't looking around. When she wouldn't budge, I stormed off and grabbed lunch. Then I went home to sulk."

Casey asked, "How long before she called, or did you call her?"

"Does it matter who called who? Or when?" Chase asked.

"Casey's establishing a timeline of events. We know the girls argued around eleven and we know they planned to meet at eight. There's a nine hour window that has to be accounted for."

Casey asked, "Gloria, did you go right home?"

"Yes. Well, no. I stopped at the grocery store and bought a ton of junk food to drown my sorrows for the afternoon. I hate fighting with Franny."

I noticed she was using the present tense. Gloria hadn't entirely accepted that Franny was gone.

"Were you home alone?"

"Yes. If you're asking if I had an alibi for the afternoon, I don't."

"Why would she need one? My sister died last night."

She tugged his hand. "Chase, these are routine questions. Please don't get so upset. Casey's doing her job."

Tipping her head, Casey said, "I'm not trying to upset you, but knowing if someone stopped by Gloria's before she and Franny talked would be helpful."

"Well, we've established she was alone."

Was he being protective of Gloria, or was there another

reason he was getting upset? I knew I had to keep a close eye on Chase during the rest of the conversation.

"Tell me what happened after you enjoyed your snack."

Bless Casey for being diplomatic. So far I hadn't needed to prompt Gloria to answer any of her questions, other than to smooth some protective feathers.

"I watched a movie, and Franny called around dinner. And we talked. A lot."

"About what specifically?" Casey asked.

"The journals, the fires, and Temperance - and then she asked me to come over. Gordon dropped off a box of cupcakes while we were talking." A smile tugged the corner of her lips. "I can't say no to a chocolate cupcake. I promised to bring ice cream but she asked me to wait and come around eight. Her friend was stopping over first."

"Do you know who he was?" I asked.

"Her new guy. I have no idea who it was. She wouldn't say."

Chase said, "I don't get what the big deal was."

"I can't answer that question," she said.

"Okay, you waited. What time did you leave your house?"

"Um. Around 7:45. I needed to get gas and I wanted to buy bait and ice cream and the Quickie Mart is on the way. I stopped in and it was quiet, which is not unusual for a Saturday night at that time. Most people are doing whatever it is they're doing. Keith and I chatted for a couple of minutes. I got my bait and two pints, which he joked didn't go together, and then I left. When I got to Franny's, I went inside."

"Where did you park?"

"In front of the garage like always. But not on the side where she parks, just in case we decided to go out and take her car."

"Why's that?" Casey asked.

"She hates my driving." Placing a hand over her heart, she said, "Hated."

"Did that bother you?"

Gloria laughed. "Not at all. I'm not the best driver, Chase can vouch for that."

He laughed softly. "Yeah, don't ride with this one if your nerves aren't steady."

I smiled. "Good to know."

"Gloria, who was at the house when you arrived?" Casey asked.

"Gordon. He'd come back to let us know that Henrietta had already submitted an article about the new little bakery and it was all from the cupcakes."

"Was Franny upset or anxious?"

"Not at all. She was happy to hear the exciting news about the article."

"Other than Gordon, was anyone else there?"

"No, just the three of us."

"Do you remember if the outside light was on when you parked your car?"

Closing her eyes, Gloria took her time answering Casey's question. "I don't remember but it would have made more of an impression if it wasn't on. Franny always turned on her outside lights before the sun finished setting."

"What time did Gordon leave?"

Running her hands through her hair, she said, "Um."

I glanced at Josie. She said, "Do you think Gordon stayed for a while longer? Maybe he had a cupcake with you?"

"No, I don't think so. I brought in the vanilla ice cream and left the Rocky Road in the car since I didn't think I'd be there that long. He volunteered to get it for me."

"Did he?" Casey asked.

Her features pulled into a pinched expression. "No. I said it was in a freezer bag and I'd get it shortly. He left out the front and a bit later I went out through the garage door." She tipped her head to the side and squeezed her eyes shut. "That's the last thing I remember until you were shaking me at the river."

I scooted forward on my chair. "Did you see Gordon drive away?"

"No?" It wasn't reassuring that she answered me with a question.

I said, "Think hard. This could be important."

Her mouth fell open as she jumped to her feet. "Oh-Em-Gee." She whirled around, clutching the back of the chair. "It can't be. He'd never hurt Franny or me. I'm his cousin."

Chase pushed back his chair and it hit the cement wall. His face was deathly pale, and his voice icy. "Are you saying that Gordon killed my sister and left you alone and bleeding at the river?"

She wailed, "He wouldn't do anything like that. Even if he burned down the greenhouse and the barn, he'd never hurt a person. The barn didn't have any livestock in it, and the greenhouse fire was during the night. No one got hurt."

"Why wouldn't he just talk to you about it? Feel you out to see what you really knew?" Josie asked.

"If he'd been listening, he'd have known who we thought was responsible."

Casey asked, "Did you say his name?"

"No. That was one rule we never broke. We never said the name, not even to each other after we read the journal," she sank into the chair. "I wish we'd never found that stupid book."

"Temperance, a moment?"

I followed Casey into the hall. She said, "If the girls didn't say the name and Gordon thought they were talking about him, he would have lashed out. I need a patrol to go by his home. If he's there we need to place him under arrest and bring him in for questioning. But give me your impression. Do you think he's capable of arson, assault, and murder?"

I exhaled and looked at the door we had just walked through. "Until Gloria said he was at Franny's, he was low on my list of suspects. But he had the opportunity to get close to them both. But why would a young kid burn down his grandparents' barn? It could have gotten out of control fast and burned the entire spread."

"But they said they knew who it was."

"Casey, Gloria still hasn't mentioned a name. For all Gordon knew, it could have been Kelly, Seth, or someone unknown."

"Who knows how his mind was working? Guilt can cause people to react unpredictably. You know that."

My shoulders slumped. She was right, I did know that. "Go set the arrest in motion. I'll stay with Gloria. Maybe she'll remember something else." I snapped my fingers. "Has anyone asked Babette if the front light was on? She seems to be very active in keeping track of Franny; it would be a detail she might have noticed when she said there was a lot of company last night."

"I'll check the report and get back to you on that. If it's not mentioned, I'll run by tomorrow and ask."

"I'm going back in."

"Thank you for your help. Everyone in the department appreciates your input. Oh, and what did you uncover at the Quickie Mart?"

I smiled. "Am I that transparent?"

"You bought ice cream and…"

"Just as Gloria said, the place was slow until around ten. Then Keith mentioned there were customers around ten pm for gas. No one paid cash. It's a long shot, and the footage is gone, but what if someone needed gas after an impromptu trip to the river? The credit card receipts could shed some light on who was in the area."

"We're checking all gas stations but the Quickie Mart is

the only chance for late night gas. However, that's a good point."

"One other thing. When you have Gordon in for questioning, ask him what bait is used for night fishing. If he mentions lures, not worms, there's reasonable doubt of his guilt."

Casey said, "I thought of that, too." She said, "I need to get things moving. Be back shortly."

When I entered the room, Josie was sitting quietly as Gloria paced the perimeter of the room. "I refuse to believe it was Gordon. It doesn't matter what that stupid journal implied. It just can't be him. If we had spoken up, he could have been cleared."

Chase's fists were clenched into tight balls on the tabletop. "He'll pay for what he's done. Not just about Franny, but you too. You might have rolled into the river and been swept downstream." He squeezed his eyes shut as if trying to get rid of that mental image. He looked at me. Daggers lingered. "We have to find out who was at Franny's last night. Jacob's mother must have seen something. She's always standing either in their living room window or on the front porch. She's a busybody and doesn't miss anything."

That was another question Casey could ask tomorrow, since I doubted that it would already be in the report. With some luck, she saw Gordon's car. "Gloria, where did Gordon park his car?"

"In the street. Why?"

"Wouldn't he have parked in the driveway?"

"Oh, gosh. Maybe he met the new man in Franny's life."

I looked at Josie and she nodded. I knew she thought the same thing, *could there be another viable suspect?*

16

Moments later, Casey entered the room. "Gloria, someone's going to take you and Chase back to your place. We've done a drive by and the bees seem to have quieted, but I suggest you keep doors and windows closed and stay indoors until the situation can be properly addressed in daylight."

"Is it safe for us to go home?" Chase asked. "You know—for the other reason?"

"Yes, there will be a constant police presence overnight, and tomorrow we'll reassess."

Gloria pulled her shoulders back. "You're bringing Gordon in to question him, aren't you?"

Casey said, "Yes. Officers are on their way to his place."

"I want us to leave before they arrive. Is that possible?" Gloria looked at Chase.

"Temperance, will you drive them home? I'll have an officer right behind you."

"Sure, Josie and I'll stay until the officer checks in."

"Thank you. Gloria and Chase, are you okay with this plan?"

They both nodded. Gloria said, "I just want to get home and eat some of that ice cream the ladies brought."

Josie smiled. "I'm not sure it'll still be frozen, but it's in a cooler, so maybe it will be."

"Come, let's get you two home. I'm sure Gloria could use some rest." Chase looked as if he was dragging too. "And Chase, do you need to stop at your place?" I glanced at Casey, who inclined her head, indicating that it would be all right.

"I'm set for the night."

"You're parked out front, Temperance?"

"I am. Josie, I'll start the car."

"We'll be right behind you."

Chase shook Casey's hand. "I know I've been difficult at times since this morning. I don't know which end is up. The world has tilted on its axis and I feel like I'm spinning out of control. Franny was my pillar of strength."

She placed a hand on his shoulder. "You have good friends in Oak Hollow. All you need to do is reach out when you need support."

His chin dipped. "Lock him up so he can't hurt anyone else."

"Trust me, Chase. We'll arrest the guilty party. You have my word."

Gloria said, "If I remember anything else, should I call you or wait until tomorrow?"

"Call the station. They'll find me."

I left the room, satisfied everything that could be done was being done. I thanked the police officer behind the desk and jogged down the steps to my SUV. A police cruiser pulled into the parking lot and around the back. A person was in the backset. Unfortunately, I couldn't make out who it was. Had they already arrested Gordon and gotten him back to the station?

I backed up and pulled close to the steps. Gloria must be

exhausted and I wanted to make this as easy for her as possible. Josie held her elbow while Chase supported her on the other side. Dark purple upside down crescents had settled under her eyes. I wasn't sure if it was bruising from the attack or pure exhaustion. It didn't matter, I needed to get her home.

No one spoke during the short trip. It wasn't until I parked in her driveway that Gloria said, "I still can't believe any of this happened. It's a nightmare and I want to wake up."

We got out and I took her house key to unlock the door. A dark colored sedan pulled to the curb.

"Wait here." I jogged across the lawn.

A tall police officer unfolded himself from the car. "Temperance Matthews?"

"Yes, who assigned you here?"

"Officer Casey Butler." He scanned the area. "I'm Officer Nate Hawkins. I'll be handling security tonight."

He was built like a linebacker on a major league football team.

He nodded at my car. "Is that Gloria Nardin and Chase Clark?"

"Yes. Josie Shaw is the other woman."

In a no-nonsense tone, he said, "I'd like to walk through the house before they enter."

"Of course. Do you mind if I come with you?"

He looked me up and down. Expressionless he asked, "You're the former agent?"

"Yes." I was surprised he knew who I was.

"You can wait inside," he said, looking at the house, "in the kitchen."

"Thank you. I'll tell the others the plan."

He accompanied me across the yard, continuously scanning. This cop didn't miss a thing. He paused. "What's that buzzing sound?"

I shrugged. "A slightly angry beehive on the property line in the backyard."

His eyes widened a fraction of an inch before returning to an assessing gaze. "Did you notice anything when you pulled up?"

"It's late and the neighborhood is quiet." Unlocking the door, I started to cross the threshold when he placed a hand on my arm, stopping me mid-step.

"Wait until I give you the all clear." The authority in his voice had me step aside and let him enter the house first.

Several minutes had elapsed when I heard, "Temperance."

I entered and discovered Officer Hawkins standing in the doorway to a bedroom. "Have a look."

I walked down the hall.

"I contacted Officer Butler and she asked me to show this to you." He crossed the room to another door which I guessed was the bathroom.

My heartbeat slowed. His face was a mask as he gestured inside the small space. Scrawled on the mirror in red was a message, *Keep your mouth shut!*

"Any thoughts?"

I pulled out my cell and took several pictures, looked around and said, "The window's ajar."

"It wasn't like that before?"

"No. When I walked around back earlier today, the slider and the living room window were open but I didn't notice this one. Chase was worried about the bees swarming. If he had known a window was open, he would have closed it." I walked in front of Hawkins and peered out. "The screen is slashed on the ground and I would have noticed that."

He depressed a button on his handset. "Officer Hawkins requesting investigators."

"Copy that. Location?"

I pointed to the door and walked into the other rooms I

was sure had been cleared. I walked to the living room, where my cooler was on the coffee table. Opening it, I discovered that although a bit soft, the ice cream could be enjoyed.

Waiting for the officer, I was about to put the ice cream in the freezer when Josie came to the door. "Gloria needs to sit down. Can I bring her in?"

"Let me check with Officer Hawkins."

There were questions in her eyes, but thankfully she didn't ask them.

I strode down the hall and stopped outside the bathroom. "Would it be all right for Gloria and Chase to come into the living room and sit down? They've had a difficult day and I'm not sure if you're aware but she has a head injury."

"This room is off limits."

He accompanied me back to the front door. "Miss Nardin, you can come in but I'll ask that you stay in the living room for the time being. I have investigators en-route."

Her face paled, something I had seen far too much of today. I took her hand and helped her up the last step, guiding her to the chair she had been in previously.

I settled her. "You should put your feet up and try to relax."

Her gaze darted around the room. "What's happened? Temperance, your face is a mask, but I wouldn't have to stay in here if something wasn't wrong."

It wasn't my place to reveal the facts.

Officer Hawkins rested his hands on his belt. "I believe while you were at the police station, someone broke in and left you a message on your bathroom mirror."

"I want to see it." There was no mistaking her determination as she pushed herself to a standing position, swayed, and demanded, "Show me."

He hesitated for a fraction of a moment. "Don't touch anything, not even the walls or door."

"Got it. Look with my eyes and not with my hands. I'm not a child, Officer."

He clenched his jaw as his eyes met mine. "Come with me."

The four of us followed him down the long hall and into what I guessed was Gloria's bedroom based on the slippers by the bed, a book on the nightstand, and the bathrobe on a hook. It dawned on me this could have happened last night before she left for Franny's but it hadn't, the screen indicated that.

I asked. "Gloria, did you leave the bathroom window unlocked yesterday?"

"It was open while I took a shower. To get rid of the excess steam, I opened it a couple of inches, but I'm sure I closed it. Why?"

Hawkins said, "The screen is on the ground slashed. It's logical to assume that's how the perp entered."

Chase said, "Which is smart since the neighbors would never be able to see anyone in the backyard."

Josie caught my eye. That would have been the same outcome for riling up the bees. Especially after dark, no one would have seen a thing. She mouthed the words, *tonight too.*

I kept my thoughts to myself, but we were on the same page, and it was something I could share with Casey later.

Hawkins nodded as he seemed to catch my idea. "Look at the message and let me know if you recognize the handwriting."

She stepped in front of him. Staring at the mirror she read the words out loud. "Keep your mouth shut." A shuddered breath escaped from her lips. "At least it didn't say or else."

Chase said, "Glo, that was implied."

She turned and pushed past us. "I've seen enough."

Holding on to the wall, she stumbled back to the living room. Hawkins frowned but there was little he could do.

After all, this was her house, so it was expected that her fingerprints would be everywhere.

"Temperance, do you know if she has home security cameras?"

I shook my head. "Not to my knowledge. If she did, I think that would have been the first thing Gloria mentioned after she learned of the threat."

"True."

A flash of blue lights whipped around the room. He said, "Reinforcements."

"If you don't need me to stay with Gloria and Chase, Josie and I will leave."

He nodded. "Sure, and keep what you saw to yourself. We don't want to alert the perp."

"He might be sitting for questioning right now."

Hawkins bent low and pointed to the lipstick case on the floor. "This isn't Miss Nardin's brand or shade. It was brought here for this purpose."

"It's expensive. Not one you can purchase in a pharmacy."

He gave me a look that caused my stomach to clench. "The perp might not be at the station."

The sinking feeling I experienced again was becoming too familiar. I snapped a couple of pictures of the case and said, "I hope you have an uneventful night."

"You as well."

I passed two plain-clothed officers headed down the hall. Gloria and Chase were on the loveseat. I forgot to ask Hawkins if I could store the ice cream, but what the heck. I pulled the pints from the cooler and stashed them in the freezer, pausing to take a quick look. Not that a freezer was expected to yield clues, however it never hurt to double check.

"Temperance, are we leaving?" Josie was in the archway.

"Yeah, Hawkins will be here and the two others are

working the scene. Gloria and Chase are safe and we need some rest. My brain is drained."

She gave me a tired smile. "Hank'll need to go out, too. Would you mind if I crashed at your place tonight? I don't feel like being alone."

"You know the spare room is ready for you anytime."

She laughed softly. "It's becoming a habit, a few nights last week and now tonight."

"Think nothing of it. Hey, when your backside imprints on the sofa, I'll start charging you rent."

This time her laugh was genuine, and it was like a salve on my jagged nerves, not that I would admit to anyone here that I was feeling the strain of the situation. I closed the freezer. "Let's say goodbye and take off."

ONCE I PARKED in my driveway, I turned the engine off and sat there staring into the darkness. "First thought that pops into your mind when I say—Gordon."

"Nerdy. Nice. Quiet."

"That was three words. But I can see how they fit. Next, Chase."

"Protective. Brother. Loyal."

I nodded. "Kelly."

"Driven. Nice. Standoffish."

"That's interesting." I tipped my head from side to side; working out the kinks in my neck. "Jacob."

"Friendly. Good mechanic."

"Just two words for him?"

Josie wrinkled her nose. "Well he, Chase, and Seth were always tight, but the three of them weren't nice to Gordon or other nerdy kids, so his friendliness extends just so far."

"Finally, Seth."

"Smart. Ambitious. Big ego."

My eyes widened as I stared out the windshield. Out of our suspects Gordon would be an easy patsy for someone like Seth. Jacob too. Kelly was driven and female. I wondered what brand of lipstick she wore?

A couple of sharp barks reached me. "Ready to take Hank for a stroll?"

Josie grinned. "That's the best medicine for an overtaxed brain, a happy little dog."

Once we had Hank on his leash, he bounded out the back door and down the shadow-filled driveway. The breeze caressed my skin and the moon had made its appearance as the clouds thinned.

She glanced at me. "You've gotten quiet. What's buzzing around your brain?"

"Call me crazy, but I don't think Gordon set the fires, killed Franny, or hurt Gloria."

"You don't?"

I heard the shock in her voice. "No. Think about it. He and Gloria are cousins. You said it yourself, he's nerdy. I'm taking a leap here, but did our other three male suspects bully him in school?"

"They did. He wanted to be a jock like them but he wasn't coordinated for sports. He was better as the water boy or team manager."

"Do you have any idea what brand of lipstick Kelly wears?"

"That's out of left field. But I don't think she wears any. Tempie, tell me what you're thinking. I can't make heads or tails of your questions."

"Gloria's a curvy girl. Would you say she's about the same height as Gordon?"

She sucked in a sharp breath and stopped walking.

When I did the same, Hank danced around my feet as if asking what the holdup was. He wanted to conduct a sniff test throughout the neighborhood.

"There's no way Gordon could have carried Gloria to the river—down the embankment in the dark."

After a brief moment, she said, "If he dragged her, she'd have other injuries, but she doesn't."

Exactly. So, either he had an accomplice or he's not guilty, which leads me to the real question: if we eliminate Gordon as the prime suspect and since I don't think Chase killed his sister and attacked the woman he obviously loves, then it has to be Seth, Jacob, and/or Kelly.

17

———

I tossed and turned and finally gave up pretending to sleep. I sat up and put my feet on the floor. Hank wriggled to be picked up from the bed and I set him down. He zipped off to the kitchen while I detoured to my office for a pad and pen. I had so many questions and flashes of half-truths whirled into a jumbled mess in my brain. I needed to write things out logically.

The smell of coffee lured me into the kitchen. I stopped in the doorway. "Josie. What are you doing up so early?" She was sitting at the kitchen table with a mug of coffee.

I propped the oversized pad against the upper cabinet and poured a large mug of steaming hot bean water. "Couldn't sleep either?"

She looked at me over the rim of the mug. "No. I don't get why Gloria blamed her cousin for the fires instead of leaving her and Franny in an overanxious state for years. If she thought he had done something wrong, why not confront him ten years ago and encourage him to talk to the authorities?"

"If the first fire was an accident, they would have gone easy on him, but add in the greenhouse fire, and that would have changed everything." I got up, letting Hank out the sliding door for him to toddle around the yard and do his morning routine.

I grabbed a box of graham crackers and placed them near Josie. "I'll fix breakfast in a bit."

"No rush." She opened the box, took a few crackers, and dunked one in her coffee. "This'll hit the spot. Are we mapping out what we know?"

"It's the only way for me to make sense of the noise in my head." I took another sip of coffee and stared at the blank paper. "Recent events started with the argument between Franny and Gloria. We were close to Chase, Seth, Gordon, Kelly, Jacob, and Russ. Even though we couldn't hear them arguing, it was obvious they were upset. But one of the others could have heard snippets of the fight."

Josie got up and wrote down the list of people as I said their names. She put a check mark next to Seth, Gordon, Jacob, and Kelly. "One of these people is most likely the guilty person."

"We can place Gordon at Franny's Saturday night. Gloria confirmed he was there and that he dropped off the cupcakes."

Gordon got another check mark.

"Even Gordon confessed to being at Franny's Saturday night. However, we don't know where Kelly or Jacob were." I tapped my chin. "Didn't Chase say he and Seth were at the drag races?"

"Yes, and I think they met Jacob there. I remember Chase talked about fast cars and Saturday nights with friends."

I frowned. "I'm not sure they met up with Jacob. Chase said he thought they would."

"At the races guys aren't joined at the hip. They might meet up and sit together for a while and then wander around alone. Seth or Jacob could easily have slipped out, gone to

Franny's and done the deed, and then made it back to the track before the last event."

She had a point, but we needed more evidence to know who was where. "Casey must have everyone's statement and verified information. We'll check with her where these guys were. The big hole in our data is Kelly Woods. Other than the fire and someone breaking into the landscaping office on Saturday night, she's flown under everyone's radar."

"Does that put her at the top of your list?"

My eyes narrowed as I pictured Kelly in my head. "She's petite. How would she have gotten Gloria to the river? That's kind of the same question we have about Gordon. He's not a muscle-bound guy."

"No but Seth, Chase, and Jacob are. They're all former high school jocks who've kept in shape."

"We can't overlook the possibility that Kelly and one of the others could be in on this plot together. "Nothing was taken at the landscape office during the break-in which occurred around nine on Saturday night, right?"

"That's what Casey said, and there was a lot that could have been easily taken and sold for decent money."

I tapped the side of my mug. "What if the killer wanted to cause a diversion?"

"To what end?" Josie asked.

"If Kelly had reported the cameras were tripped at nine, police officers would have been dispatched immediately. The medical examiner thinks Franny died around ten. She was probably stung earlier since anaphylaxis can take from fifteen to sixty minutes to succumb. In that time frame, the killer could have knocked Gloria out and taken her to the river, leaving Franny alone. Remember the vanity drawers looked as if they had been opened but not fully shut, the same with the medicine cabinet?"

"Could Franny have been looking for another EpiPen?"

I cocked a brow. "It's what I'd do. I'll bet the killer took them." I rushed from the room, took my cell off the charger and hurried back to the kitchen. "Chase said he found her on the sofa, but how? Was she sitting as if she were watching television?"

I tapped a message to Casey. "Breakfast? Josie and I have questions." I spoke as I typed and looked at her before I hit send. "How's that?"

"Good."

"We should make a list of questions for Casey. Start with — was there anything taken from the break-in at Twigs? Next, how was Franny positioned on the sofa? Who was Kelly's date, and where did they go? Where is Franny's cell phone? Did they find more EpiPens?"

Josie was writing as fast as I rattled off my questions.

"Where was Gloria's cell, in her car?" I paused. I paced to the slider and whistled for Hank to come in. He trotted to his water bowl and then sat down, giving me the expectant look of, *breakfast?*

My cell pinged. I read the text from Casey out loud. *Be there around eight.*

"That's good news," Josie said, "What else is bothering you?"

"It's too bad about the security cameras at the convenience store. If we could have seen who got gas later that night, it might be useful since it's the only station in town open that late."

"Add that to the list for Casey - credit card receipts."

She underlined that question. "This is important, I can feel it in my gut."

I nodded. "Me too." Other than staring at the paper with the same thoughts going nowhere I said, "How about we make a massive breakfast? It'll get our minds off the cases."

"Are you still thinking we should pop around to Twigs and Petals today? I know you said it might be a great opportunity to poke around."

With a smile I said, "We'll do that after breakfast and our round of twenty questions with Casey. We could happen to bump into Kelly and see what we might uncover from her, like who she's dating and what she thinks the motive was for the break-in, and we can try to move this investigation forward. We're in a great position to turn over rocks and find nuggets of information for the police."

"You're so confident that we can help."

Hank barked, wagging his tail. I picked him up and nuzzled his soft ears. "What do you think, should we exude confidence to make it happen?"

He barked again, his tail beating against my side. I laughed. "Hank has faith we can pull this off."

"In conjunction with Casey's investigation."

"You've seen and heard everything she's said. The Oak Hollow PD welcomes our help with the case." I frowned, "To be honest, I'm not sure why they've been willing to let us in the loop."

She chuckled. "Think of it this way. If the late, great James Beard offered to come to your kitchen and give you bread-baking tips, would you let him?"

"I'd be moronic if I didn't." *Cartoon Temperance had a light bulb go off over her head.* "I'm James Beard in this situation?"

"Yup, and the police are more than happy to allow you to analyze clues."

Protesting, I said, "I was a data analyst."

"Tomato. Tomahto. Information is relevant to each aspect. You take the data in, dissect and think about it every way possible, and come to a logical conclusion. Then you pass along that information to Casey or Sergeant Franklin to follow up on. The end result—you've helped."

She had a point, not that I liked being compared to a field agent. I knew I didn't have the chops to handle that job. Well, except for a few times.

"I guess. But this just gives my mind much-needed exercise. I don't want to get stale. Which is why I do crossword puzzles and other mind games to stay sharp."

"And it's working." She slapped me a high five. "We should cook. What are we making for breakfast? You know Casey will be starved and can eat enough for two people."

"Whatever you're in the mood for - frittata, pancakes, waffles."

Her eyes gleamed. "You clinched the case at waffles."

"You fix the batter, and I'll make a frittata. Let's get crackin'" I snorted, "Eggs that is."

AT FIVE MINUTES AFTER EIGHT, I heard a tap on the back door. Casey walked in wearing her uniform, with her short, dark hair slicked back. Before she said hello, she asked, "Any chance there's coffee?"

I gestured to the pot and mug I had left for her. "Help yourself."

"Thanks. These last few days have blended together, and I'm bone tired."

I quirked a brow. "You, super cop, who can operate on almost zero sleep?"

"I know, right? It's this case. I was sure Gordon was guilty, but when I asked him about night fishing, he launched into an entire speech about lures and fish. To be honest, I never want to hear about anyone fishing at night again." She slumped in the chair and took a slurp of coffee.

I grinned. "It was that bad?"

She nodded and sipped again, this time silently. "By the way, thanks for the tip."

Josie gave me a smile as I said, "You're welcome."

"We released him with the caveat that we have eyes on him. He protested his innocence and said he'd be a model citizen. Other than going to work he was staying home, alone."

"At least it will be easy to track his movements should anything else happen with the case."

She tipped her head from one side to the other. "What's for breakfast? All I've had is coffee and a pack of sawdust-tasting donuts from the vending machine since dinner."

That was one way to change the subject from the case.

Josie said, "We've got oceans of coffee, waffles, frittata, crispy bacon, and OJ."

"Sounds good." She stood and opened the cabinet for plates.

It was nice to have good friends who were comfortable pitching in. Maybe that's why Casey was chill about having me work on the case with her, trust.

After she placed the plates and silverware on the table, she poured juice. As she moved around the space, I kept a watchful eye on her. Something was brewing, and I'd give her time to talk about it. In the short time we'd known each other, we'd fallen into an understanding. Patience was the key.

"Doesn't it feel like we've known each other for years?" I asked.

Josie said, "We have, but pulling Casey in does seem like we've been friends forever. Hey, it's like we're peanut butter, jam, *and bread*."

I snorted, "I'll take the bread since I bake; Josie, you're sweet like jam and Casey's the peanut butter."

She gave me a side eye. "Are you implying I'm a nut?"

Laughing, I said, "Heavens no. You stick, which is a good thing."

With a thoughtful nod, she said, "Good analogy, Josie. Not one I would have chosen but still appropriate."

Laughing I said, "PBBJ Trio. Or maybe it should be PBJ."

Josie grinned. "Just one B. It sounds better."

I was hopeful that the light-hearted conversation would loosen Casey's thoughts. We sat down to plates of steaming food.

Shooting a glance at Josie, I said, "We're planning some landscaping for my front yard, since there isn't anything we can do with the case until the medical examiner's report is available."

"Really?" Casey smiled as if she knew what we were up to. "Temperance, would you do me a favor? It's unusual, and under different circumstances, I might not ask, but… how do you feel about talking to Kelly Woods? She's hiding something. If you're at the garden center to hire landscapers to enhance your new bakery cart — especially since everyone trampled your flowers on Saturday — she might open up to you and Josie. You're the friendly faces of her neighbors and you're part of the business community. It's natural you'd be concerned about her since you heard about her trouble."

I didn't have to look at Josie. She had to be thinking the same thing I was. It dovetailed perfectly with my plans. "Sure, Casey. We'd be happy to help. Is there anything specific you'd like us to try and discover?"

"Who was her date? Where did they go? And if she is lying about equipment that might be missing from the office and the shop. We still can't confirm if Seth, Jacob, and Chase were at the races as they claim, or if they had an opportunity to sneak over to Franny's house, and well, you know."

Like me, she was tired of talking about a young woman's murder and another woman's almost murder. Josie dropped her chin. It weighed on her too.

"Casey, you can count on us." I wasn't sure what I could say to get Kelly to reveal everything, but with Josie and me playing the concerned friends and fellow business owner, we'd find a way. We had to, Gloria's life depended on it. On that, I was certain.

18

---

*J*osie parked her car in the parking lot of Twigs and Petals. Our mission: seek out Kelly Woods and find out who she was on a date with, why she thought the office had been broken into, and what she remembered about the fire.

I looked at Josie and gave a curt nod. "Ready?"

She grinned. "You were born to do micro spy missions."

"I'm not sure about that, but I do have a unique set of skills and you're the sweet one in our dynamic duo. Don't underestimate what you bring to the table." We stared out the windshield at the array of potted flowers on wooden benches in front of us. "How do you want to play this?" A plan was important so we came off as natural.

"We'll start out shopping for plants. Considering it's Monday, the center isn't busy and Kelly should be around. It'll be natural for her to come and chat and you can take it from there."

It sounded simple enough. As long as Kelly was working. We got out and walked around the hip-high fence to stroll among the flowers. "These are perennials?" I held up a pot of pink flowers.

"Those are begonias, an annual. They're great for a spot of color, you'd need to plant them every year."

I put it down. "I want to plant and forget it." I did this a few more times, casually scanning the open area, in hopes that my lack of plant knowledge would garner help from the owner.

Finally, our patience paid off. Kelly circled the perimeter and it wouldn't be long until we crossed paths. She smiled when she saw us.

"Josie, Temperance, hello."

"Hi, Kelly," I said. "Would you have time to talk about plants?"

Her smile widened. "I'd be happy to. What are you looking for exactly?"

"That's just it, I'm not sure. Did you know I'm converting an old flower cart into the new bakery stand in my front yard?"

"I didn't realize you were using an old flower cart, that's a charming idea. But, if you're filling it with baked goods, where do flowers fit in?" She glanced at Josie. "You're a gardener, I'm surprised you didn't chime in with some ideas."

"If the gardens were established, I would, but Temperance wants to create a landscaped area as a backdrop for the front yard so it's not just about the bakery stand. The area should have a cohesive look. I suggested we stop by to see what she likes and maybe talk with you since you're the real expert."

Kelly beamed. "Ah, that's nice to hear. After this past weekend, I could use a shot of positivity."

I gave a sympathetic nod. "We heard about the trouble you had Saturday night. Did they steal much?"

She pursed her lips. "That's the funny thing. I've checked that building over three times and I can't find one thing missing. It must have been kids pulling a prank."

Josie asked, "Did I hear that you didn't notice the security camera had gone off until later?"

Rolling her eyes, she said, "That's true. I thought I was on a date with this guy but it turned out he thought it was a business dinner. Like who goes out to dinner, all dressed up with a handsome man on Saturday night to talk business?"

"Ouch," I said. "How did those wires get crossed?"

She leaned her hip on one of the flower displays. "A local contractor in town met me for dinner at Bistro 9. Earlier in the week, we'd been talking about a new project for the garden center. I suggested we meet for dinner to talk more about it. He's a terrific guy, and I thought he was interested in me. Boy, did I get those signals wrong." She looked around, but we were alone. "I kind of made a fool of myself."

"How?" Josie took a step closer and touched her arm. It was the right amount of concern. I was impressed but knew it was genuine on her part.

"It was about eight. We had appetizers and drinks, and our dinner would have been served soon when he pulled out a small notebook from his shirt pocket. He started talking about the project. I had the entire evening planned —twenty questions on postcards, like you have at speed dating, so we could get to know each other better. You know I ask a question, he answers it, and then I answer the same question." Her cheeks flushed. "When I handed him ten cards, he glanced at them and asked me what they were for. In his defense, he was a gentleman when I told them they were getting-to-know-each-other questions. I thought it would be a good icebreaker for us to move beyond customer and contractor. When he placed them face down on the table, I knew something wasn't right."

Was she talking about Russ Patterson? I glanced at Josie whose sole focus was Kelly. "I'm sorry. How did he handle the situation? It must have been awkward."

"Oh it was. Dinner was served and he grew quiet. Once

the waiter left, Russ was sweet. He told me I was a terrific person but he never saw me as anything more than a friend. There's a woman he's interested in and he's still working up the courage to ask her out." Her chin dipped and color reached her cheeks. "Then he asked if he should leave. He didn't want to make the evening more uncomfortable for me." She placed a hand over her heart. "Can you imagine?"

"Then what did you say?" Josie asked.

"I extended my hand and said, hello my friend, please stay and have dinner with me. I hate dining alone."

"And he did?" I glanced at Josie. I was dying to know if he named the other woman.

"We finished dinner and had a great evening. He's got a great sense of humor and we talked about the new building I want constructed near one of the greenhouses. He said it was something he'd like to bid on if I would accept it."

"I'm glad it worked out. What time did you leave the bistro?" I asked.

"Almost ten. That's when I noticed the cameras had been triggered. I called 9-1-1 and met the officers out here." She glanced over her shoulder.

Josie asked, "Did Russ mention who it was that had caught his eye?"

"No. But she's a lucky girl. I was dressed to the nines, and for him to turn me down when I made it clear I was interested in him, she must be something special."

Josie gave me a sly wink. "I'm sure she is."

At least Russ hadn't bruised her ego. "After you got here, you didn't notice anything amiss?" I asked.

"Nothing. Someone had to know how to get around the gate via the back part of the property that borders the woods. It's the only way and they must have used an ATV to get in and out quickly. There wasn't even a broken window. The door to the building was open so they had to have a key."

That was a tidbit Casey didn't mention. "If I understand

correctly, whoever came in via the woods must have known where the security cameras were and how to avoid them?"

"That's correct."

That sounded more like Chase than our other suspects. "And you're positive nothing was missing?"

She shook her head. "I'm as surprised as you are. It's the weirdest thing. Like why go to all the trouble of coming here, getting in the building, and leaving without so much as a trowel?"

"Who has keys to that particular building?" I had to move cautiously, lest I remind her too much of the police questioning.

"Chase and Gloria have keys. They are heads of the landscaping crews. Franny had a key since she was the manager. There's a key in the main office and of course I have keys to everything."

Josie asked, "Did you check to make sure the office key was still there?"

Her brow furrowed. "I never mentioned that key to the officers when they were here. Maybe we should check." She stood and took two steps before looking over her shoulder. "Are you coming?"

I nodded. Josie fell into step with her. This was great information, even if the key was in the office; all that she shared was important. Although my mind drifted to Russ saying there was a woman he liked but was working up the courage to ask her out. I pushed those thoughts aside. I had other things to occupy my brain.

We walked through the automatic glass and metal doors past the cash register area and moved to a side door at the end of the aisle. She tapped in a code and ushered us up the stairs.

"How many people know the code to access this area?"

"All the cashiers and a good portion of the staff in the center. About twenty people, give or take."

She crossed an open space to a large work table. Underneath was a cabinet. She withdrew a key from her pocket and unlocked it. Without words, she rummaged inside. Finally, a small smile appeared. Holding up a key ring she jingled it. "All the master keys are accounted for. Whoever got into that building used Chase, Franny or Gloria's key."

I knew Gloria and Chase were both off for the day. "Has anyone returned Franny's work keys to you?"

She bit her lower lip. "No, and I never thought about them until now. Should I call the police station and ask them? The keys are a bright green color."

"You do color coded keys too?" I asked.

She laughed. "I take it you have the same system?"

"I did until the Early Rise burned. The employees had one color, Josie had a master along with me. It helped us figure out who started the fire."

She nodded. "That was good, but since my key is here, this won't be useful information."

It would if Chase or Gloria's keys were missing. But I didn't say this; it was confidential to the investigation.

"We should get back to discussing plants and your plans. Do you want to do the work yourself, Temperance?"

"Heavens no. I can water them and pick flowers when they bloom, that's the end of my garden skills."

With a soft laugh, Kelly smiled. "In a few days, after things have returned to normal and my staff is back, how about I stop over? We can look at the areas for these new gardens, what exists today and develop the next steps."

"That's perfect." I extended my hand. "Thank you for your time, and I'm sorry it didn't work out with Russ."

"To be honest, I'm not. The way his eyes lit up when he talked about that other woman made me realize I want that too."

"Kelly, I was surprised you stopped to see Seth on Saturday."

"Oh. That." She exhaled. "When he was at the garden center a few days ago, he dropped a credit card and I brought it over." The office phone rang, and she said, "I need to get that. Just make sure the door is secured when you get downstairs. I don't want customers wandering up here looking for a bathroom."

I wanted to ask what day but I'd let Casey follow up on this bit of information.

Josie waved goodbye as we crossed the room. She whispered. "That went well."

I nodded and pressed a finger across my lips. We could talk freely once we were outside, preferably in her car.

The motor was running when Josie turned in the driver's seat and looked me in the eye. "What's next?"

"Back to my place. We have some great information for Casey, but you know, let's swing by Gloria's just to see how she's feeling. With a bit of luck, we might even be able to ask about the green keys."

Rubbing her hands together, she said, "Great idea. We'll be there in five minutes; do you want to call Casey?"

"I will. Who do you think Russ was referring to when he mentioned there was a woman he was interested in? He kind of asked me for coffee. So, I must not be the person?"

With a quick glance, she asked, "Do you want to be that woman?"

"I didn't think so, but hearing he was at dinner with Kelly, as a business thing, I got a twinge of regret that I wasn't across the table from him."

"Sounds like you're interested. Be ready for when that man asks you out and plan on saying yes."

"Maybe it's you."

"Doubtful." She grinned. "Now if Erik Wool asked me out, I wouldn't be able to say yes fast enough."

I laughed. "Maybe you should ask him and not wait."

She smirked. "Maybe I will."

I called Casey and she answered on the third ring. I felt bad when I heard her groggy voice. "Casey, it's Temperance. I have you on speaker, Josie's driving."

"Hi, how did it go at Twigs?"

"Great. Mission accomplished."

"I knew sending you over was the right decision. Tell me what you discovered."

"Her master key to the landscaping office is secured, and there are three others besides hers. Franny, Chase, and Gloria are the only other ones who have green keys. Can you have someone check at the station and see if they have Franny's keys? We're on our way to Gloria's. With some luck, we'll find out about theirs."

"I'll contact the station when we hang up. Anything else?"

"Yes, Kelly thinks an ATV was used to gain access to the property through the woods and they used a key to unlock the door."

"Interesting, anything else. What about her date?"

"It was a working dinner with Russ Patterson. That'll be easy to verify. She said they got to Bistro 9 around eight. And left by ten."

"Excellent. You wrapped up all my questions. How about your landscaping?"

"Kelly will stop by in a few days, and we'll come up with a design, and Casey, I don't think she suspected that we were investigating."

"I never doubted your ability, Temperance. We'll talk later."

I had enough doubts for the both of us.

19

We drove past Gloria's, but the house was locked up tight. Chase's truck wasn't in the driveway, and I knew the police still had her car as evidence. "I guess we'll need to check in with them later."

She sped up. "Back to your place?"

I turned in my seat. "Are you up for a slight detour?"

"Always. What do you have in mind?"

"What if we took a trip back to the river? I want to see if I can find that bait box, the one that was on the trail and then wasn't. It might be a clue as to who was near the river when we were."

"We might have missed it. My adrenaline was pumping when we were searching that area."

She turned on her blinker and headed back to the river. Looking out the window watching the trees blend one into the other I knew what I saw. Maybe Josie was right, and in the excitement, it was overlooked. A bait box might be nothing, or it could clinch the case.

When we pulled into the small parking area we saw Chase's truck. At least we knew where they were.

Josie parked and we were perched at the top of the hill

looking down. I didn't see them but if they were at the beachy area they'd have walked through the trees.

"Do we search for the box first or the beach?"

I didn't want to alert anyone of what we're doing. "The box first, then we can find Chase and Gloria."

Moving slowly, we sidestepped down the steep incline. Josie said, "How could anyone think Gordon got Gloria down this hill is beyond me."

I scanned the area. "Is there another access point?"

"If you go down river, you'd have to walk through the woods, water, and brush to get to the beach." Her mouth gaped open. "Do you think that's how someone got her down there?"

"It's possible. Can you show me after we're done?"

"Of course. Should we call Casey?"

"After we've searched the wormhole. If we bump into anyone suspicious we'll leave, contact Casey, and then you can show me the alternative route upstream."

We had reached the bottom of the hill and went down the path. It was wide enough for us to walk side by side. I moved slowly, with my head down and my eyes scanning from right to left. In some areas, the path was wider, and in others, more narrow, but it was always bordered by tall grass and small bushes. We reached the wormhole, and I walked to the water's edge. It was peaceful beneath the tree canopy. Why hadn't Gloria been dumped here?

Josie's shoes were off, and she had waded into the water. "You should cool off. The water gently wafts around you and it won't drag you down."

"That answers one question I had."

Placing her hand above her eyes to shade the small amount of sun, she asked, "You didn't say anything."

I shook my head. "I wondered why Gloria wasn't left here but when you mentioned the current, if the attacker wanted her to get swept away, this wasn't the right spot." I pointed to the trail. "We should head back." The sharpness in my voice wasn't directed at her, but the frustration I felt about that stupid bait box. If it wasn't here, someone had been lurking and took it, for what purpose was hard to say.

We were halfway up the path when two boys raced in our direction, fishing poles and tackle boxes in hand. I recognized them, they were the same kids who took a box of cupcakes.

I said, "Hey boys, what's the rush? The fish will still be in the river when you get to the wormhole."

"Hey, Ms. Matthews," Billy skidded to a stop. "I told Jeff that when I came down to fish on Sunday. I found a bait box full of the best night crawlers right on the ground. I was kinda hoping it'd happen again. I only get scrawny worms from my backyard."

"You were here on Sunday?" I glanced at Josie. "I didn't see you."

He bobbed his head. "Yup. I came down to see if the fish were jumping and found the box of night crawlers right next to the path. So, I ran back up to my bike and rode home to get my stuff."

"Did you take the bait with you?"

"Sure did. You can't leave that kind of treasure just lying around. Unfortunately, when I got home Mom made me do my chores so I couldn't get back to the river until after lunch but the worms were still good."

"The important question," I grinned, "did you catch anything?"

"I sure did, a twelve-inch trout." Smacking his lips, he grinned, "Good eatin' too. I told Jeff we had to come back and see if we can catch dinner again." He glanced around, "Any chance you found another box?"

"Sorry, not today. You boys be careful fishing."

Jeff said, "We will. Our moms know we're here. We can't fish from the beach part; the current gets too fast so the wormhole it is."

Josie said, "Have fun and good luck."

"Thanks!"

With a shake of my head, I chuckled. "Sometimes the simple explanations are the best."

"Leave it to a kid to think a box of found bait is a treasure."

"It's all about perspective." We walked through the stand of trees separating the beach from the path. At the water's edge, Chase and Gloria sat in beach chairs, fishing poles in hand, toes in the water. I gave Josie a poke. It was a peaceful picture of a couple enjoying the moment.

"Hello." I called to them.

Chase turned in the chair and lifted a hand in greeting. He said something to Gloria, who took off a large-brimmed sunhat, and stood. "This is a surprise."

"Hi Gloria. We wanted to look around."

Josie said, "I'm surprised to see you here."

She dropped her head before looking up again as she removed her dark glasses. "I asked Chase to bring me back to the beach. This has always been my happy place and I didn't want what happened to drive me away. That maniac took my best friend, but I won't let him take anything else from me."

"Are you sure it's a him?"

She nodded and put her glasses back on. "I remember being carried. My head hurt so bad I couldn't focus. I know he carried me like a sack of mulch over his shoulder."

"Do you remember any smells, like cologne?"

"I don't think so. Other than a metallic kind of odor."

I placed a comforting hand on her arm. "It's ok." Do I tell her that smell was likely from her blood—iron meeting oxygen?

Josie asked, "Are you doing okay?" She nodded to the chairs.

A small smile tweaked Gloria's lips. "Chase is a rock. This

was his idea to come back, and I've caught a couple of small fish and released them. Balance will be restored eventually."

On impulse, I gave her a hug. "You'll feel better once an arrest is made."

Chase got up when he heard me and asked, "Are they close?"

"I'm not able to share specifics because I don't know any but we had breakfast with Casey this morning at my place and they're closing in. I'm confident it will happen by the end of the week."

"That's fast," he said.

"The police are good at their jobs," Josie said. "You get back to fishing and we'll see you later."

He took Gloria's hand. "I'll take care of Glo, not to worry. She's safe with me. Besides, her bodyguard is in the tree line."

I swiveled in the sand and sure enough a woman was standing at attention in the trees but not the same person we met last night. I waved. That made me feel better about them being down here.

Josie said, "Good luck. Oh, and Billy Moore and Jeff Collins are fishing at the wormhole, just in case you hear them carrying on. They're hoping to catch supper."

Gloria smiled, "Aren't we all?"

At the top of the hill, I called Casey and left her a voice-mail. "Josie and I are at the RR. She mentioned a way to walk up the river to the beach area that's easier to traverse than the slope from the parking area. We're going to check it out and let you know what we find."

"We can leave our car here, but I'll show you where you can tuck a vehicle out of sight from the road." Josie strode down the street, and I ran to catch up.

"You're on a mission."

"Every minute that ticks by without an arrest hurts my heart even more."

My heart ached that she was struggling. She'd been solid

over the last weeks. I couldn't ask for a better friend. "Josie, how about we go to dinner tonight at Bistro 9? My treat."

"A night out sounds great and having a delicious meal is even better. When we're done sleuthing I'll go home, take a long hot bath and meet you there at what time?"

"Six. I'll make a reservation."

"A girl's night out is exactly what we both need right now."

That was my thought. We came around the bend in the road. Josie pointed to an overhang of trees where a small dump truck could fit in without being seen, especially at night. I took several pictures to send to Casey.

There was a narrow path, barely wide enough to walk single file. Josie took the lead, placing each foot carefully so as not to disturb the brush on either side. Once we were deep in the thicket, a strip of green cloth stuck to a bramble caught my eye.

"Josie, hold up." I took a bunch of pictures and sent it to Casey with a text. "Need CSI team stat," and gave her the location. "We need to wait by the road and not go any further. This fabric is from Gloria's ripped T-shirt."

"Are you sure?"

"Without a doubt. If we continue we could contaminate important evidence." I looked down the path and longed to keep going. However, the best chance for an ironclad case was to let the professionals do their job. "We need to go back to the road and wait."

We made our way back. This time I took the lead and we traveled the short distance with our hands in our pockets, being careful to keep our clothes from getting torn. My cell pinged with a text.

Once in the sunlight I read it. "Casey said to hold tight, she and others are on the way. And she said good special detective work on our part."

"That's us, sleuth extraordinaire." Josie sat on a fallen log and dropped her head in her hands. "Temp, I get why you left the FBI even if you weren't in the field. Being immersed in this world of crime, murder, and assault can wear on a person."

I sat next to her and placed an arm around her shoulders. "It can, but you discover how to create balance and chase the shadows with the sun. Hence dinner tonight is our ray of sunshine in an overcast day."

With a nod, she said, "Even though this has been the second hardest thing I've ever been a part of, I'm glad I'm able to help."

Squeezing her shoulders, I said, "I couldn't have gotten this far without you."

She laughed. "That's not true, but thanks."

A HALF HOUR LATER, police cars swarmed the area. A CSI van and Casey's truck claimed prime real estate. Casey strode over and handed me a note. "A copy of the credit card receipts from the Quickie Mart on Saturday night."

Scanning them, I said, "Russ got gas around ten. Is it ok if I check with him and see what I can find out?" *That's odd, the amount's double what I'd think his truck would need.*

"I was hoping you'd offer and let me know when you do. I was on my way to his job site when I got your text. This search is more important. If we can find physical evidence to tie it back to the attacker, we're that much closer to an arrest."

Hawkins jogged over. He gave me and Josie a curt nod. "Butler, we're ready. Are you coming?"

She looked at Josie. "If we take this path down, we'll walk past what?"

"You end up at the top of waterfalls. Then if you walk about one hundred yards or so the beach will start to come into view. Casey, if the person used this path they knew exactly what they were doing. The current should have taken Gloria over the falls."

"Good to know. We'll touch base later." She and Hawkins walked away and didn't look back.

"We need to talk to Russ. Care for another side trip before you drop me at home? Hank will need to stretch his legs but first I want to make a reservation for dinner. Hopefully, they'll have a table at six."

I called the restaurant and luck was on our side. Someone answered and confirmed that a table was available. Putting my phone away I smiled, "All set."

Josie said, "I texted Russ for you. He's at the bakery doing one final inspection. The clean-up crew finished and he'll wait for us."

"Good." I leaned against the seat and closed my eyes. Gloria had said she was carried like a bag of mulch, slung over a shoulder. For anyone to have carried her like that they'd have to be strong. With the distance it could be done, even if he shifted her from one shoulder to the other. Chase, Seth, or Jacob were all capable.

The vehicle stopped. I opened my eyes to a vacant lot where my bakery had stood ten days ago. It had bustled with activity, customers coming and going buying my breads, cookies, muffins, and cupcakes. My heart constricted that a senseless act of revenge had cost me my life's work to this point. Like a phoenix I would rise from the ash.

"There he is, Mr. Handsome." Josie pointed to where Russ was. She tapped the horn. He looked up, waved, and grinned.

"Patience, Josie."

"Are you kidding? To have him flash that grin in your direction is worth the noise."

"Stop. You're incorrigible."

"And you're in serious interest mode."

I poked her arm. "Stop. He's coming over."

He walked to my side and I slid the window down. "Hi

girls, this is a surprise. Temperance, did you want to look around?"

"Hey Russ, it looks good but that's not why we're here. I need to ask you a couple of questions, if that's okay."

He gave a nervous chuckle. "Sure. You sounded like a cop just then."

"Sorry." I felt my cheeks grow warm. "Casey showed me receipts from the Quickie Mart on Saturday night. You got gas?"

He nodded. "Yeah, it must have been ten, or ten-fifteen. I had gone to dinner with a client and stopped to fill up. I used my credit card. I know Keith doesn't like dealing with cash later in the evening."

I nodded, noticing he said he was having dinner with a customer, not a friend or a date. "Did you see anyone that you knew also getting gas?"

"Sure. Gordon was there. He was between pizza deliveries and I saw Jacob. I was surprised to see him. Earlier he, Seth, and Chase were talking about going to the races."

"Did you talk to him?"

"Yeah, we were at the same pump, opposite sides. I noticed he had mud on his boots and his pant legs were wet. When I asked him about it, he said he was looking for a friend's dog down by the river. I offered to help, but he said the pup had been found and was at home getting a much needed bath and cookies."

"Do you remember what time that was?"

"Hm. Must have been ten-fifteen. I'd been there for a couple of minutes waiting for a pump when he pulled in." His eyes narrowed. "Why?"

"Just curious. Did you see anyone else you knew?"

With a shake of his head he said, "Just a few people towing campers and a couple of boats."

Josie said, "That's interesting, don't you think, Temperance?"

"One last question, did Jacob pay with cash? I didn't see a credit card slip for him."

"Funny you should mention that. He couldn't find his wallet and asked if I'd float him a fill up and he'd catch up with me today. Of course, I didn't mind, he's a stand-up guy," he chuckled, "and I know where he works."

"Do me a favor, Russ. Don't tell anyone about this unless it's the police. Forget everything."

His smile dimmed. "Temperance?"

I shook my head. "Sorry, I can't say anything more but we'll talk soon."

"If you say so. I'll swing by tomorrow and check on the kitchen."

"Sounds like a plan. See you then." He walked away and I called Casey. She had to hear that Jacob just ramped up on the suspect list and that Josie and I were going home to relax for the rest of the afternoon.

"Hey Casey. I talked with Russ."

"And?"

I told her everything and my thoughts on the lost dog.

"Great work. "We're on it. Don't worry. We'll bring Jacob in for questioning within the hour."

"Good luck. If you make an arrest, it'll put Gloria's mind at ease."

"Temperance, I gotta run. I'll catch up with you later," she disconnected.

"That's a wrap, Josie. Time to take the rest of the day off and pamper ourselves before dinner."

She grinned. "I like how that sounds."

ON THE SHORT drive to Bistro 9 my cell rang and it was Gloria.

"Hi there. How are you feeling?"

"Hi Temperance, would you mind stopping over for a quick minute? I could use your advice."

"Now?" I glanced at the dashboard. If I did, I'd be late for the dinner reservation.

"Please? It would mean a lot and seriously I only need like sixty seconds."

There was a quiver in her voice that constricted my heart. Flicking on my blinker, I did a U-turn at the intersection. "I'll be there in ten minutes."

"Thank you, Temperance - and hurry." The line went dead.

I pulled into the driveway, noticing the front door was open. I left the SUV door unlocked and hurried to the house, slipping my cell in my back pocket. Tapping on the door casing, I eased the screen open. "Gloria, it's Temperance."

An oversized hand clamped on my wrist and dragged me inside, shoving me into the living room. Gloria was cowering on the opposite side of the space, her eyes wide with fear and her cheeks damp from tears.

Jacob slapped the blinds closed. "Now we can talk. In private."

20

———————

*J*acob filled the doorway, with a handgun leveled at my chest. Gloria was behind me, trembling. Her fear was palpable. My arms were outstretched as a barrier between him and her, but they offered no protection if he lunged at us, or worse pulled the trigger. In a calm, reassuring voice I said, "Talk to me. Maybe I can help."

"The only way anyone can help me is to never say a word about the fires or Franny." He scanned the small living room, taking note of the back door. His eyes never blinked.

"We won't say a word. Gloria and Franny kept your secret for years."

His eyes locked on mine. A cold shiver raced down my spine when he slammed the front door shut. I quickly realized this wasn't a situation I had trained for, and I'd have to rely on my wits to get Gloria and me out of this unscathed.

"It's too late for that. Someone," he jabbed his finger in Gloria's direction, "got a case of the guilts. I kinda figured that was happening which is why I took Franny out a couple of times, to determine just how trustworthy she was."

Gloria said, "She would have kept the secret forever."

"That's not what I heard at Temperance's house. After Chase and I emptied the last loads of plaster in the dumpster he went back inside and I waited around the corner out of sight. I heard you girls arguing about coming forward. I knew everything would be lost if I didn't talk to Franny and convince her to keep quiet about the greenhouse fire."

"Then why did you kill her?" I locked eyes with him.

"That was an accident."

I slipped my hands in my back pocket and hoped I'd successfully record the conversation. If the worst happened, I needed to leave evidence to help the police solve all the crimes. "Really? She died while she was enjoying a cupcake with her best friend. How did you come into the picture?"

"I guess it doesn't matter if I tell you. After tonight, everyone will think you went back to Virginia. Gloria will back me up, won't you?"

Her voice was shaky, "Sure, whatever you say, Jacob."

His smile held no warmth. "Sit down."

"No, thank you. I prefer to stand." Also, if someone passed by the house they'd see my silhouette in the window and know we were inside.

"Suit yourself."

"Why frame Gordon?"

He shrugged. "He had the best chance of getting off scot free. No one would believe he was guilty of burning his grandparents' barn down. And he's got zero muscles; he couldn't have overpowered Gloria and taken her to the river. Gloria, you should have let the current take you downstream. That was a slight miscalculation on my part."

"You wanted me to die?"

"I didn't need you as a witness if you remembered what happened or decided to tell the police about the fires. We don't have a statute of limitations on prosecution in this state. If it's any comfort, I didn't want to *actually* kill you. I thought drowning was peaceful and given how much you love to fish

I thought it was fitting, which is why I left your fishing equipment on the beach as a memorial to you."

It was interesting that he knew the laws. "What kind of bait is used for night fishing?"

"Don't know. Don't care." He narrowed his eyes. "Why do you ask?"

"Just curious." I wasn't about to give him any details he might use later to wriggle out of charges.

Now that I knew why he chose Gordon, would he tell me how Franny died? Besides knowing it was a bee sting.

"Where did you get the idea about a bee sting killing her?"

"I've always known about Chase's reaction to them, and when I saw the EpiPen on the table next to her that night, it was an obvious solution. Especially since she mentioned Gloria had a huge nest at her place and if Glo held any of her fun picnics she wanted to be prepared, just in case."

Gloria said, "You made a bee sting Franny so she'd die? What kind of monster are you?" With each word, her voice got louder.

Jacob grabbed for her arm but Gloria wrenched away at the last moment. "Answer me!"

"Of course I didn't hold a bee to her skin and tick it off so it would sting her."

"Then how did it happen? There weren't any obvious welts on the body from the medical examiner's report."

"Funny story." He took one look at me glaring at him and said, "Well maybe not so funny. Anyway, I knew what kind of bait Gloria bought at the Quickie Mart. So I bought some and dumped the night crawlers out. Then I filled it with water and sugar to lure a few bees into the case. That took all afternoon but I managed to get some nice specimens."

I asked, "How did you get the bee to sting her?"

"That was an accident. Franny and Gloria were sitting in her living room sipping wine and eating cupcakes when I dropped by for the second time. I pulled the tub out and shook it. The little buggers did their job and let out a warning buzz. Her face went from the glow of health to the paleness of death. At this point, she hadn't been stung."

"What did Gloria do?"

"Told me to get the bees out of the house because Franny was deathly allergic, and what was I thinking?" He smirked. "I only meant to tease her and use the threat to convince her to keep her mouth shut."

Gloria said, "That's when she told you to get out of her house. She said she never wanted to see you again."

I whipped around. "You remember?"

She nodded. "Franny chased him out the door and threw a book at his head. It missed and broke the outside light."

"That woman had pretty good aim. I had no idea or I would have recruited her for the town's softball team."

I rolled my eyes. How could he trail off and talk about a team when he was confessing to killing one woman and attacking another?

"That's when the oops happened." He lifted his shoulder. "In my defense, if she hadn't thrown the book at me, I wouldn't have missed the top step, and the lid wouldn't have popped off. Franny lunged to shove me the rest of the way down the steps and, like out of a novel, she swallowed a bee." He laughed, but it wasn't pleasant; there was an ugly undertone, almost as if he enjoyed what he was about to tell us.

"Why didn't she use her medication?"

Gloria jabbed her finger in his direction. "He raced into the house and grabbed it off the table, then went back outside and threw it on the ground, lifted Franny into his arms and carried her into the house before he dumped her on the couch. I raced to the bathroom to get another one, and he wrenched it from my hand."

Her face was deathly pale and I was concerned for her.

Her voice cracked. "Jacob, you wanted Franny to die."

"It solved one problem. Do you remember what happened next?" A muscle pulsed in his clenched jaw.

She scowled. "I'm not sure." Tipping her head, she said, "I went to the garage to get an EpiPen from her car."

He nodded. "I followed you, saying I was sorry and that I'd help look for another one. When you got out there, you were confused how your car got inside. I had eased the car inside before I came into the house. You and Franny were so busy yacking, you missed the door opening and closing. I told you my mother and grandmother were always watching, and they'd think you'd hurt Franny because of your feud, which I had casually mentioned earlier in the day. You bought it." He tapped his temple. "Gotta think ahead just in case."

Her mouth hung open.

He said, "You turned, I whacked you in the back of the head with a wrench and put you in your car until I could take care of things inside the house, like doing the dishes. Franny would have been so upset if the police came and saw they weren't done. For the record, that tool will never be found. I have the most amazing hiding places all over town. But you already know about those since you found my journals."

"You thought of everything, didn't you Jacob?" I asked.

He beamed. "Kind of. I'm pretty proud of myself. Well, not carrying Gloria out into the current was a miscalculation on my part. Who knew she wouldn't just roll into the water?"

He moved like a cheetah stalking prey, slowly, inch by inch, as if I or we wouldn't notice. "Where's Gloria's guard?"

"Not to worry. When she wakes up under the honey tree, she'll have a nasty headache but she'll be just fine. Trust me."

I snorted. That was ironic. "Like Franny was?"

He brandished the gun in my face. "Be nice."

"Tell me about the fires, oh, and did you do something to the bees out back?" I had to stall and ask every question I could think of since I wasn't armed and there was no way I could wrest the gun away from Jacob; he out-muscled me with his pinky. Where in the heck were Hawkins and Casey?

"The bees? Yeah, I tossed a bunch of rocks at the hive just to get them stirred up and it worked. Too bad Chase heard the humming, that might have been epic.

"Regarding the fires, there's nothing to tell. Other than I was working for the Nardins that summer, and Pops Nardin was tough to work for. One day he pushed me too far. He wanted me to clear out the loft before we started haying. Have you ever done a job like that in the sweltering heat? My friends weren't busting their backs like I was for the same amount of money. I wanted to quit but my parents had this thing about finishing what you started. I had to work for him for the summer." He shrugged. "I finished the summer early. There's more than one way to leave a job on decent terms. I helped rebuild the barn so I was part of the hero crew. No more long days that went from sun up to sun down. Working in construction, you start early and quit early to avoid the heat. I had plenty of time to hang out, swim, play ball - you know, the good life."

It was hard to believe that this was the same guy who willingly helped at my house just two days ago. "And the greenhouse?"

"More to see if I could get away with it. I felt bad for Kelly's family, but they had insurance, and look at how she spring-boarded the business to even more success. I did them a favor."

He waved the gun at us and then pointed it at the basement door. "It's time, ladies. It'll be quick, and Gloria, I'm going to make it look like Temperance killed you and then herself. It's the least I can do since I botched your previous attempt at a watery grave. Your reputation will be clean as a whistle."

"Wait, why did you break into the greenhouse last night?"

He lowered his head briefly. "You're a smart lady. Maybe

you should have stayed with the FBI, but yeah, that was me. I was trying to create a diversion. At that point, I didn't intend to kill Franny. I just wanted to scare her and Gloria and let them know I could get to them at any time so they would keep quiet. I rode in on the ATV, unlocked the door, and left. I didn't steal one thing and managed to avoid all the cameras."

"Where did you get the key for the door?"

He nodded at Gloria. "She keeps her keys on the rack inside the kitchen door and when she was watching a movie Saturday afternoon, I snuck in and took them. That's when I checked out the bee hive. Double score for me."

The entire time Jacob was talking, I was trying to find the best way out of this situation. The only idea I had was to hurl the coffee table at the front window, but with the shades pulled I'd have to throw it with every ounce of strength I could muster and hope the glass would break.

"Wait!" I cried.

He groaned. "Why are you stalling? I promise it won't hurt. I'm an excellent shot."

How about that I didn't want to die? "Did either your mother or grandmother see you Saturday night here?"

A deep scowl creased his face. "What makes you ask that? It's not like they'd turn their flesh and blood into the cops for murdering anyone."

"Wouldn't that make them an accomplice to not one but three murders?"

"Look. I had no issue with you until you got involved in my business. Now, you ask way too many questions and have become collateral damage. Let's get something straight, you and Gloria need to shut up, walk through that basement door and down the stairs into the game room."

He turned the knob on the basement door. I grabbed the coffee table, hoisted it over my head, and threw it as hard as I could against the glass, shattering it. I grabbed Gloria's arm. "Run!"

Before I had finished saying the word, she leapt over the footstool and raced to the front door. I was right behind her. Jacob grabbed my hair and hauled me back.

"Wait," he growled. "We're not done."

The shade was ripped from the front window. Josie pointed a revolver at Jacob. I had no idea she owned a gun but I'd never been so happy to see her face.

Her eyes locked on Jacob, "Let. Her. Go!"

"Josie, mind your own business." He swung the weapon in her direction. I stomped on the arch of his foot and smacked my head against his chin as hard as I could. Shaking off the stars that whirled around my head, I shoved him with the remaining strength I had against the wall. The basement door burst open and Casey came out, shocking everyone.

The momentary stunned state was just enough time for Hawkins to burst through the front door. He and Casey said, "Freeze!" in unison.

She continued. "Jacob. Drop the gun and put your hands up."

Hawkins approached him. "Don't make any sudden moves." He gave me a side glance. "Are you okay?"

I nodded, not trusting myself to speak. Pointing to the door he said, "Go outside and wait."

Josie guided me to the maple tree next to the driveway. Gloria was in an animated conversation with Sergeant Franklin, while Babette and Hattie were speaking with another officer.

Hugging her I asked, "What took you so long to get here?"

She tipped her head. "No one was sure where you were since you weren't at the bistro. Chase called and asked if Casey could do a wellness check on Gloria. He got stuck with a flat, and she wasn't answering her cell. She tried to call you and when you didn't answer, she called me. Then I tried and it went right to voicemail. I called Casey back and she said she was coming over. I decided to meet her here."

"When did you arrive?" I pressed a hand to my throat, feeling my pulse race, and took several slow, cleansing breaths.

"I heard most of Jacob's warped explanation, and you did a great job of keeping him talking. The table through the window—genius."

I gave her a weak smile. "Hopefully, Gloria won't hold that against me. And since when do you own a gun?"

She held it up. "This? It's a toy I used with my costume for Halloween last year. I was Annie Oakley."

I started to laugh - softly, at first, and then it grew into a deep belly laugh. "Oh, Josie, only you."

A WEEK LATER, Josie, Casey, and I were sitting on my front porch. Hank snoozed in his comfy little bed next to my chair. It was the first opportunity we had to talk since Jacob Heffner had been arrested for the fires, Franny's death and Gloria's attack. He was also responsible for the break-in at Twigs and Petals *and* holding me and Gloria at gunpoint, with the intention of silencing us permanently.

"Temperance, how's the construction project coming along?" She leaned forward and looked at the piles of building supplies lining the driveway.

"Great. Russ has a fantastic crew, and Chase and Seth have been by to hang drywall. With all that happened, I thought they'd stay as far away from me as possible."

Josie said, "Nothing that happened was your fault. Don't give it another thought."

"Casey, did Jacob say how he got Gloria to the river?"

"It was like we thought, he transported her in his truck, stuffed her sweatshirt in the bushes as another red herring that she had gotten hurt at the river. He burned the drop cloths he used from Fanny's place. We have no idea where the wrench went, but he admitted to slipping into Gloria's house and leaving the message on the mirror and he cleaned up the dishes at Franny's after he abandoned Gloria. His grandmother came forward, saying she saw him later that night, sneaking out of Franny's around midnight. It took her a few days to contact the police."

"I get it, he's family," I said.

Josie said, "They did the right thing in the end."

"Whose lipstick did he use and why leave that note in my future bakery? It made zero sense."

"The lipstick was taken from a customer's car at the garage." Casey's lips tipped up. "The note was a mistake Jacob made. He had no idea where he dropped it and when I showed it to him, his face went all shades of purple and he demanded to know where I found it."

We sipped our lemonade. Casey glanced my way. "Are you sure you don't want to join the force?"

"Nope. Private citizen Temperance Matthews."

Josie laughed, "I'll bet you can count on Temperance to jump into the fray again if it ever becomes necessary."

I shook my head. "Not likely. This is a charming little town. There's been enough murder and mayhem to last twenty-five years. My lofty goal as of today is to perfect my walnut double chocolate brownie recipe."

Casey gave me a side eye and licked her lips. "I'm available as a taste tester."

"As the owner of a little bakery, I'll keep that in mind, I said. "But my full-time job is perfecting recipes—and that doesn't leave time for a side hustle of solving murders. Case closed."

Little Bakery Cozy Mystery Series
Book Three
Walnut Brownies & Murder
A Temperance Matthews Cozy Mystery
LUCINDA RACE

SNEEK PEEK - WALNUT BROWNIES & MURDER

Chapter 1

I scooped lemon bar batter into the baking pan, carefully swirling lemon zest ribbons across the top. The soft launch of the Early Rise 2.O took place this weekend, and the engagement party for a local couple needed to be a smashing success. No pressure at all.

Looking up, the kitchen door banged shut. My best friend, Josie Shaw, entered and flopped on a stool with a theatrical groan. She ran a hand through her currently blonde hair, brushing it from her gray eyes. "I'm exhausted."

My brow arched, but I didn't look up. "Hello to you, too." I pointed to the coffee pot. "Need some go-go juice?"

"Nah." Josie exhaled and dropped her head to the counter. "If I drink another drop, I'll never sleep tonight. I've hit the twitchy eye stage of caffeine overload." She lifted her head. "Whatcha baking?"

"Right now? Lemon bars. I've completed the tiny cheesecakes, petit fours, and mini tarts. After these, the frosted double fudge brownies with walnuts will round out the dessert trays."

"And this is for the Carmichael Posey party?" She wrinkled her nose as if those names were distasteful.

"That's right," I slide the pans into the convection oven and set a timer on my phone. "Why the sour face?"

"I'm not sure how it's been for you to deal with them, but after I got the invitations finalized and at the printers," she threw up her hands, "Wendy Carmichael changed them. Again. And now she wants the Posey crest to be incorporated into the design."

I washed my hands and turned, giving her my full attention. "There's a Posey family crest? I thought they were just a normal, wealthy family."

"Right?" She slapped her hand on the countertop. "Apparently, the Posey family claimed the crest in the 1700s before they left Hampshire, England, with nothing but a trunk of linens and silver."

"Are they descendants of nobility?"

"I doubt it's historically factual. Something like that would have come out by now on the Oak Hollow grapevine. Honestly, it's Wendy putting on like she's Lady Posey or something." She tipped back her head and pressed her fingertips to her eyelids. "She's the client, so I'll redo the darn invites for a third time, but what a waste of time and money."

"As long as you get paid, that's the upside."

She shot me a knowing grin. "Yeah, that's the one way to look at it. How's Wendy been with you, frosting on a cupcake or vinegar and salt?"

With a laugh, I said, "A cupcake with vinegar frosting."

She laughed. "Upside for you, Temperance— the Oak Hollow Hideaway Inn might become a regular customer."

I crossed my fingers and looked at the ceiling. "From your lips…"

She leaned over the counter and ran her finger over the inside of the bowl, scooped up lemon batter, and licked her finger clean. "This is so good. Any chance you'll have an extra lemon square, brownie or three?"

Bobbing my head to the hand-wash sink, I chuckled. "If you help, you can take a plate home with you."

WOOF. Hank's bark carried from the other side of the door leading from the commercial kitchen to my home. "Sounds like my fur baby needs a break." Tossing the towel from my shoulder to the workbench, I crossed the room.

My hand hovered over the doorknob.

Josie joined me. "I've said it every day for the last two weeks, this kitchen is awesome. Not only did Russ do a fantastic job, but he finished in record time."

"It's pretty great." I glanced at the gleaming stainless steel counters, the bank of ovens against the back wall, the four-burner range next to the sink and dishwasher, and shelves on every open wall space. "The layout is perfect. Baking in here has been better than the brick-and-mortar storefront that burned down." I gave an involuntary shudder when I thought of the fire that changed the course of not just my life but also the lives of three others.

Josie touched my arm. "It was a tragedy, but you have a fresh start."

"True, but there are events I wish had turned out different-ly." I pushed the door open, Hank, my black and tan dachs-hund, was waiting patiently. His head tipped from one side to the other as he barked again. I scooped him up.

"Hank, you're a good boy." I kissed the top of his head and checked his water and kibble bowls; both were full. Josie slid open the glass door, and he wriggled to get down.

We followed him outside. He pranced around the grass, his nose twitching as he inspected every inch as if he'd never been outside before. I chuckled. "Hank, do your business."

He ignored me. "We might as well sit and tell me how you're going to incorporate the Posey crest into the invitation."

Josie perched on the top step, and I settled next to her.

She said, "It's going to be straightforward. I'll add it to the center top and have it on the return address flap on the back of the envelope."

"What's it look like?" I pulled the ponytail holder from my hair and rubbed the back of my head.

Withdrawing her cell, she tapped a few keys, then handed it to me. "Blow it up. It's actually kind of cool."

I zoomed in as she suggested. "It's a coat of arms, not a crest. See the four quadrants?" I held the phone up for Josie.

"The top left is a blooming rose bush, probably to signify the family name, Posey. The top right is a key crossed with a feather quill." Pausing, I tried to remember what they symbolized. "The key is for hidden knowledge and the quill represents the legacy."

Josie peered closer as I talked. "The bottom left is a ship. That must represent their journey to America."

"What about the last quadrant, the tree stump with the new leaf coming from it?"

I narrowed my eyes and peered closer. "A new beginning, but look just above the symbol. There's a book sealed with a single rose in the wax. *Veritas sub rosa.*"

Her voice was filled with awe. "Is that Latin?"

I tilted my head toward her as I handed over the phone. "Yes, it means *truth beneath the rose.*"

"How mysterious," she whispered as she scrolled over the image. "Do you think there is a hidden meaning?"

"It's hard to say. However, like you said, the name Posey is associated with flowers. Maybe the book also represents knowledge. Without searching it and the family history, I can't pinpoint the exact meaning."

"It will add a nice touch to the invite, but I wish Wendy had asked for it before the printers had done the run."

I gave her a shoulder bump. "It'll work out. I'm surprised she hasn't asked me to create a stencil and design a cake."

Josie guffawed. "Give the bride-to-be a moment. It's not every day you get to micromanage the world wearing white silk."

I slapped my hands together and threw back my head in laughter. Hank stopped, stared at me, and then barked before racing to my side. My little sidekick never wanted to miss out on the fun.

I rubbed his velvety ears. "Hank, don't you think Josie's clever?" He barked and wagged his tail as if he agreed.

My phone vibrated as the timer went off. "I need to check the lemon bars." Carrying Hank inside, I closed the door and set him on his bed. "You be a good boy; I'm going back to work."

He lay his head on the blankets, eyes pools of melted chocolate, and looked as if he had just been denied cheese.

"You'll be fine," I reassured him.

Josie opened the adjoining door and the moment we stepped inside, the aroma of citrus and sugar filled the air. I quickly washed and dried my hands before slipping into silicone oven mitts. "Golden yellow and perfectly set," as I pulled the cake tester from the center. "A dusting of confectionery sugar and these will cool."

Josie tied an apron on and washed her hands. "Ready, chef."

"Hardly a chef, just a simple baker." However, her comment made me smile.

"What can I do?" she asked.

"The brownie recipe is on the next page. Would you start to gather the ingredients?"

"Of course. How many dozen do you need?"

"Eight, so we need to quadruple the recipe."

"Aunt Lottie's Double Fudge Brownies." She gave me a side glance. "This recipe isn't from your aunt Penny?"

"No, it was my great aunt's on Penny's side. It's the best

brownie recipe I've ever had, and brownies are my weakness."

"Did Wendy indicate this was a nut-less event?"

"She said there were zero allergies and to bake all my treats as I normally would."

My cell rang. I pressed the speaker button. "Hello, 2.O. This is Temperance."

"Thank heavens you answered. Temperance, this is Wendy Carmichael, and I need your help. Would it be possible to drop everything, go to Andrew's parents' house, and pick up platters for tomorrow? I just spoke with Eunice Moss at the inn. She doesn't have enough to display your tiny dessert station. I just don't know what I'm going to do. I still have to get my nails done, pick up my dress from the cleaners, and, well, there aren't enough hours left in today to get it all done. Are you still there, or did you hang up on me?"

I winked at Josie. "Wendy, I was waiting for you to take a breath. So why don't you take ten seconds and do four or five deep breaths?"

"There's no time. Will you help me or not?" Hysteria tinged her words, and I clicked off the ovens.

"Of course. Josie's here, and she can drive out with me, and we'll drop them at the inn. Is there anything else you need?"

Her next words came out in a rush. "You'll do it?"

Calmly, I said, "We're happy to help. Is there anything we should check on at the inn, since we'll be there?"

"Just make sure the desserts will have a nice display. But you're not taking them over today, you'll still deliver tomorrow?"

"I will be at the inn by eleven."

"Make it ten. Just to give yourself plenty of time."

I smiled, hoping it would be evident in my tone. "Wendy, this is a special time for you and Andrew. Your event planner should be dealing with the last minute details, not you."

"I know, but currently he's at another gig and I'm trying to relax, but it's hard."

I heard her fingers snap. "One last favor? Remind my future mother-in-law that she needs to bring the painting of the family crest. I'd like that hung over the buffet table."

Josie mouthed, *Why?*

"That's sweet that you're incorporating the crest into the invitations, too. But I'm confused. Isn't the buffet table outside under the tent?"

"Minor details. It's important for people to know the Posey family is growing and will remain a significant part of this community. I have big plans once Andrew and I are married."

Josie threw her arms wide. I could almost hear her say, *See what I mean?*

"I'll pass the message along. I need to tidy the kitchen and we'll head over."

"Thank you, Temperance. Andrew was right when he suggested calling you for help. If there is any question about the platters, give me a ring. I'll be on my mobile."

She disconnected, and I grinned. "Mobile? Who even says that anymore? That expression's like from a decade or more ago."

"What did I tell you? A bridezilla of the worst kind. Not only is she firing off orders to us, but I can't even begin to imagine her dealing with anyone who's on site tomorrow."

I held my hand up. "I'll be there. She asked. I said I'd help keep the buffet filled. It's only for a couple of hours. Also, I plan to have stacks of business cards in my apron in case someone asks about my petit desserts."

Josie shook her head and laughed. "Did you have to make the engagement party cake, too?"

"No, thank heavens. She wanted something similar to her wedding cake, so the event planner is in charge."

Since my bakery was destroyed, I had stopped taking

orders for fancy cakes. If I continued with my little bakery, I wouldn't ever go back to the cake business. Besides, brides were temperamental, and delivering works of art in cake form was nerve-wracking.

Josie stashed the flat of eggs in the refrigerator. "Can we leave the dry goods on the counter?"

"Yeah. I'll grab my keys and meet you outside."

I jogged to the front door, locked up, checked on Hank, who was snoozing, and left through the commercial kitchen. Josie was standing next to my SUV.

"Did you bring extra business cards?"

I patted my shoulder bag. "Never leave home without them. I should have asked; do you have time to ride with me?"

"Yeah, it won't take more than an hour or so to redesign the invites. Besides, Eunice was sprucing up the porch and the gardens for this party and I want to see the result."

I laughed and got into the driver's seat. Josie buckled her seat belt and smiled. "Wendy asked her to create a tidier space for the event."

After I was driving up the street, I glanced at her. "She's bold. I'm sure it was lovely already."

"It was." She added the address to my GPS for the Posey house and the second stop for the inn. "Like my grandmother used to say—she's bold as brass."

It wasn't long before we reached the Poseys' blacktopped driveway. It was lined with maple trees, interspersed with sections of split-rail fence draped with climbing roses.

"Impressive," I murmured.

Josie grinned. "Wait. You haven't seen anything yet."

The driveway curved gently and, around each bend, a surprise was revealed. On the left, a small orchard— trees heavy with ripening fruit. To the right, a pristine tennis court, an Olympic-sized pool, and, beyond them, a row of immaculate horse stables marking the entrance to an oversized paddock.

I gave a low whistle. "We haven't seen the house yet."

"You will." Josie pointed out my side of the car.

Just over the hill, peaks of a roofline grew larger. "Do they live in a castle?"

She laughed. "Not quite. It's a family compound. There are wings for each adult member of the family. I've heard that after the wedding, Andrew and Wendy will move in. His mother has had an entire section of the house renovated for them."

"That's quite a wedding present, and no mortgage to start a marriage. Even better."

We turned left and the brick and board façade of the house rose in front of us, all three magnificent stories. A wide wrap-around porch graced the front, although I couldn't see how far it extended down the side. Luxurious flower pots spilled over with a riot of colors and trailing ivy. I sucked in a breath. "This is spectacular, and it's been in Oak Hollow for how many decades?"

"Try centuries. According to the historical society, the original structure was built in the late eighteenth century when the family arrived from England. Apparently, expanding its footprint has been a family hobby ever since. Andrew's mother, Cissy, is an avid horsewoman and added the stables when she married Andrew's dad."

I parked and peered out the windshield, gazing at the Posey family home. "I can understand why Wendy is putting on airs, but her family is wealthy, too."

"Nothing like this. Mr. Carmichael is self-made; there's no generational wealth there. He's a lawyer and now a judge, and his wife is vice president at Oak Hollow Bank, and it's rumored she'll become president in the next few years."

The front door opened. An older woman with short, chicly

styled hair, in slacks and a blouse, crossed the porch and waved.

Josie said, "That's Cissy Posey. Andrew's mother."

I rubbed my hands together. "Let's get the platters, and I have to ask her about that painting for Wendy, too."

A FREE STORY FOR YOU

Have you enjoyed Cupcakes & Murder? Not ready to stop reading yet? If you sign up for my newsletter at www.lucin darace.com/newsletter, you will receive Cookies & Capers, which is the start of Lily and Milo's adventure, as my thank-you gift for choosing to get my newsletter.

Cookies & Capers

I stood in front of the old wood and glass door as I pocketed the keys to the Cozy Nook Bookshop. Aunt Mimi had signed her bookstore over to me. She said it felt like giving me her baby. But I loved the shop as much as my aunt did. We had worked together for the last twelve years. After attending the University of Maine, I had a degree in history and education. I had always wanted to be a teacher, but jobs were scarce and after substituting for a few years, I moved back to my home-town of Pembroke, Maine, and Aunt Mimi hired me as soon as I unpacked my suitcase.

Spending time with my aunt, learning the business, had

been the best experience. I offered to buy the shop when she wanted to retire, but she wouldn't hear of it. As long as she had free books for life, and her long-term boyfriend Nate, she said it was a fair deal. From my point of view, I had built-in backup for years to come.

Now that I was the bookshop owner, Aunt Mimi was no longer coming in every day which meant her cat, Phoenix, wasn't either and the space felt empty without a kitty lying in the window or skulking about as kitties do. I was off to the Pembroke Animal Palace to see if I could find a match.

It was a short walk in the bright noonday sun. The spring air from the ocean carried a tang of salt, but the breeze was refreshing. I waved to one of my best friends, Gage Erikson, as he drove past in his police-issued sedan. My heart fluttered in my chest.

He was a detective on the force. Not that we had much crime in our small seaside town. But one of these days I was going to get brave and tell him I had been carrying a torch for him since we were in ninth grade. What's the worst thing that could happen? We'd still be best friends, right?

I continued down the brick sidewalk, waving to William North from the Sweet Spot Bakery. He was sweeping the area around the small bistro tables in front of the bakery. William was wearing a large pristine white apron and a wide smile. A deep inhale confirmed my suspicion. He was baking cookies. My mouth watered. I did a half turn and went back to where he was finishing up. "Good morning, William." I bobbed my head in the shop's direction. "What is that tantalizing smell?"

He held open the brightly polished glass door. "One of your favorites, Lily. Chocolate chip and pecan cookies. Can I interest you in one before you continue on your mission?"

I gave him a side-look. "Mission?"

He chuckled. "Over the years my Lulu had said you had two speeds, strolling and purposeful. Just now it was purposeful so hence you're on a mission."

"I'm going to the shelter, hoping to find a kitty. The shop is lonely now that Phoenix is home every day with Aunt Mimi, and I think a cat napping in the window adds an air of serenity to the place."

"Unless you're allergic."

He had a point, but I was not willing to be deterred. I smiled. "I'm always happy to deliver to a customer." I leaned over the glass bakery case, like a kid pressing her nose against the candy case. "You made sugar cookies too and frosted them?" I sighed. I was going to need to exercise more if he continued to bake all my favorites. He was smiling at me as I looked up. "Are the chocolate pecan ready?"

He wiggled his eyebrows. "I have a tray cooling in the back."

"Then can I have one of those and a sugar cookie, but to go?"

With a flick of his wrist, he snapped open a white bakery bag and called over his shoulder. "Jerilyn, would you please bring out the last batch of cookies?"

I heard a muffled, coming, and smiled. "It's good that Jerilyn stayed on." I said nothing about his beloved wife Lulu. Rumor had it she was ill and not doing well.

He nodded. "It is. She's a hard worker and excellent with the customers."

Jerilyn bustled in from the back room carrying a large stainless-steel tray. It was lined with parchment paper and cookies the size of the palm of my hand. It was going to taste so good with a hot cup of tea later.

William put two in the bag, along with two sugar cookies, and then he handed it to me. I paid for my cookies and thanked him. "Stop by the shop later. You might just get to meet my new fur baby."

"Sounds like a plan." He grinned and crossed his arms over his rounded midsection. "You're more like your aunt than you realize. Ever since she opened that bookshop, she's had a cat, too."

I paused, tucked the bakery bag in my tote, and with my hand on the door, I turned and gave him a wide grin. "And now it's time I carry on the tradition." With a jaunty wave, I called, "Wish me luck."

Cookies & Capers is only available by signing up for my newsletter – sign up for it here at www.lucindarace.com/newsletter

LOVE TO READ?

**All ebooks and paperback copies can be ordered from my
website at:
Shop at Lucinda Race**

Cozy Mystery Books
A Temperance Matthews Cozy Mystery
Just Desserts & Murder
Cupcakes & Murder
Walnut Brownies & Murder

A Bookstore Cozy Mystery Series
Books & Bribes
*It was an ordinary day until the book of Practical Magic conked Lily
on the head, causing her to see stars. Then she discovered that her
cat, Milo, could talk.*

Catnaps & Crimes
*The fun continues as Lily practices her magic and needs to
investigate another murder.*

Tea & Trouble

Love to Read?

A fall festival, reading tea leaves and a few clues propel Lily into a new murder investigation.

Scares & Dares
What goes wrong at a haunted house is anything but expected until Lily starts following the clues.

Holidays & Homicide
Can Lily solve a murder before it ruins the holidays?

Leprechauns & Larceny
Will a dead leprechaun take the shine off the wedding?

Magicians & Murder
When four magicians roll into town for a show more than fun is on one person's mind.

Artifacts & Amulets
Milo has been keeping secrets, which can be deadly.

Cranberries & Criminals November 2024
Whose half-baked idea was it for bookstore owner and witch Lily Michaels to enter an amateur baking contest in her small town of Pembroke Cove, Maine?

Broomsticks & Blooms
The time has come for Lily to learn to fly.

Fishing & Forgery April 2025
A simple Sunday fishing adventure with friends where Lily and her friends reel in the big one.

Wands & Weddings May 2025
Lily and Gage are ready to tie the knot. But what's up with

the coven's council? Can Lily unravel this new mystery before she says, I do.

Covens & Clues October 2026
Pages & Potions
Legacy & Lies

Ghostly Gowns Series
A Paranormal Ghost Cozy Mystery Series
Ghost and Gowns
Buttons & Burglary
Pleats & Poison
Ribbons & Robbery July 2026

Cowboys of River Junction
Second Chances in Montana
Twenty years later, Renee and Hank are back where they fell in love, but reality is like a spring frost, and is a long-distance relationship their only option for their second chance?

Stars Over Montana
The cowboy broke her heart, but he never stopped loving her. Now, she's back ready to run her grandfather's ranch…

Hiding in Montana
Can love flourish while danger lurks in the shadows?

Moonlight Over Montana
From the smoldering ash, she realizes he's all the family she and her daughter need.

The Sandy Bay Series
<u>Sundaes on Sunday</u>
A widowed school teacher and the airline pilot whose little girl is

determined to bring her daddy and the lady from the ice cream shop together for a second chance at love.

Last Man Standing/Always a Bridesmaid

Barrett

Has the last man standing finally met his match?

Marie

Career-focused city girl discovers small town charm can lead to love.

Price Family Romance Series

Breathe

Her dream come true may be the end of his...

Crush

The first time they met was fleeting; the second time restarted her heart.

<u>Blush</u>

He's always loved her but he left and now he's back...the question, does she still love him?

Vintage

He's an unexpected distraction, she gets his engine running...

<u>Bouquet</u>

Sweet second chances for a widow and the handsome billionaire...

Last Chance Beach

Shamrocks are a Girl's Best Friend

Will a bit of Irish luck and a matchmaking uncle give Kelly and Tric a chance to find love?

A Holiday Romance

Holiday Heart Wishes

Heartfelt wishes and holiday kisses...

<u>Holiday Heart Wishes</u>

Hockey, holidays, and a slap shot to the heart.

<u>Christmas in July</u>
She's the hometown girl with the hometown advantage. Right?

<u>A Secret Santa Christmas</u>
Christmas just isn't Holly's thing, but will a family secret help her find the true meaning of Christmas?
The Sugar Plum Inn
The chef and the restaurant critic are about to come face to face.
Holiday Romance Box Set
Sweet with a touch of heat holiday romance novels.

It's Just Coffee Series
The Matchmaker and The Marine
She vowed never to love again. His career in the Marines crushed his ability to love. Can undeniable chemistry and a leap of faith overcome their past?

The MacLellan Sisters Trilogy
Old and New
An enchanted heirloom wedding dress and a letter change three sisters' lives forever as they fulfill their grandmother's last request to try on the dress.
Borrowed
He's just a borrowed boyfriend. He might also be her true love.
Blue
Will an enchanted wedding dress work its magic one more time?

McKenna Family Romance Series

Lost and Found
Love never ends... A widow who talks to her late husband and her handsome single neighbor who has secretly loved her for years.
The Journey Home
Where do you go to heal your heart? You make the journey home...
The Last First Kiss

When life handed Kate lemons, she baked.
Ready to Soar
Kate will fight for love, won't she?
Love in the Looking Glass
Will Ellie's first love be her last or will she become a ghost like her father?
Magic in the Rain
Dani's plan of hiding in plain sight may not have been the best idea.
After All These Years
February 2025
Arielle Clark is a famous artist with a painful past. When her first love comes to town, ghosts from the past are resurrected. But can the embers of love still linger after all these years?

SOCIAL MEDIA

Follow Me on Social Media

Like my Facebook page
Join Lucinda's Heart Racer's Reader Group on Facebook
Twitter @lucindarace
Instagram @lucindaraceauthor
BookBub
Goodreads
Pinterest
YouTube

ABOUT THE AUTHOR

Award-winning and best-selling author Lucinda Race is an avid fan of fiction. As a young girl, she spent hours reading cozy mystery and romance novels, getting lost in the fun and hope they represented. While her friends dreamed of becoming doctors and engineers, she dreamed of becoming an expert at crafting captivating novels.

As life twisted and turned, she wrote nonfiction but longed to return to her true passion. After developing the storylines for the McKenna Family Romance series and the Paranormal Cozy Nook Bookstore Series, she decided to start living her dream. Her fingers practically fly over computer keys. She weaves paranormal cozy mystery stories and romance with guaranteed happily ever afters.

Lucinda lives with her two little dogs, a miniature long-haired dachshund and a shitzu mix rescue, in the rolling hills of western Massachusetts. She's immersed in her fictional worlds, writing mystery, suspense, and romance novels or reading everything she can get her hands on.